SAMIRA SURFS

RUKHSANNA GUIDROZ

ILLUSTRATIONS BY

FAHMIDA AZIM

For the tender place in our hearts that we all call home.

KOKILA
An imprint of Penguin Random House LLC, New York

Visit us online at penguinrandomhouse.com

Library of Congress Control Number: 2021931136

Book manufactured in Canada
ISBN 9781984816191

1 3 5 7 9 10 8 6 4 2

Design by Jasmin Rubero
Text set in Fiesole Text Family

COX'S BAZAR, BANGLADESH

JANUARY 2012

INSIDE OUR HOUSE

Our house, made of bamboo
chopped by Baba's bare hands,
sits on a hill with other houses
just like ours.
The roof is crinkly blue plastic,
noisy in the wind,
hot in the afternoon sun.
Rain drips through its holes,
making dirt puddles
on the ground.

Inside, we have a single room
for the four of us.
Mama and Baba's sleeping mat
covers one corner.
Close by, Mama's silver pot
and Baba's old spit cup,
stained red from his betel leaf.

Khaled stores a cricket bat
in his corner.
Next to it, on the floor, is

my brother's blue notebook.
He tucked it in the waistband
of his longyi
and brought it all the way from
Burma.

What's mine is a stool that holds
my special blanket,
Nani's gift to baby me.
It's torn and frayed,
but when I brush it against my skin
on cool winter nights,
me and Nani are together again,
cheek to cheek.

My stomach twists
when I think about
what little
made it here with us.
But things don't make a home.
Family does,
even those still in Burma.
Nani and Nana do,
even though they are gone.

EGGS

Our eggs go *plop-plop* into water,
bubble and mist as they simmer
in Mama's silver pot.
When they're ready,
she spoons them out
and sets them in my bucket.

Our livelihood lies between
these brittle white shells.
My job is to sell
as many hard-boiled eggs as I can
to beachgoers
in Cox's Bazar.

Each oval brings
money to my palm
and food
to the bellies
in my family.

SALT

Last night, Baba said,
"If you sell all your eggs, Samira,
we can buy extra salt to keep."
He was squatting on the floor,
wrapping coconut, fennel, and nuts in betel leaf.
It's his favorite treat.

A spiral of joy rose in my belly.
Salt crystals transform Mama's dahl.

Beneath my crossed legs,
the prickly straw mat
suddenly felt smooth.

A bucket of eggs
turns into bundles of taka
turns into pinches of salt
turns into mouthfuls of joy.

I send out a wish
to sell all my eggs.
Come extra hungry to the beach, tourists!

SCOOT LOW

Every morning,
a narrow milky stream
of drip-drop pouring cha
tumbles from high
to greet me.
This is how Mama pours it.
Moments with her at dawn
bathe our day in sweetness.

Baba is the first to leave.
Shrimping is early work.
Next, Khaled,
to clean dishes and tables
for the café at Seaview Hotel.

Mama kisses me on the cheek.
"Stay safe, Samira," she says.
I'm the last to go.

Low, low I scoot,
zigzagging

down our sneaky steep hill.
My walk is filled with
sky, wrapped in pearly indigo
air, crisp and still,
and birds chirping
every morning.

KNOWING

I step past the woods
to meet a wide stretch
of golden-gray sand.
The beach goes beyond where I can see.
Khaled says it's the longest in the world!

Café doors creak open.
Outside, whining
packs of stray dogs
beg for food,
waiting for scraps
that miss the rubbish.

Fishermen throw out nets
for their daily catch.
The sea, sparkly in the morning sun,
breaks in little waves near the shore.
My eyes follow their slow, gentle peeling.
My ears tune in the gentle roar
of water tumbling on sand.
It sounds like water lapping at a boat,
like the one we boarded to cross the river

when we left Burma,
just me, Khaled, Mama, and Baba,
and Nani and Nana.
The others stayed behind:
Hasina Auntie, Jamal Uncle,
my cousin Shoba,
and my best friend, Sahara.

It's been three months
since the river tossed our boat,
our chests sinking, stomachs plummeting.
Water can be dangerous
and beautiful at the same time.
For now, I stay as far away
as I can.

A BETTER LIFE

In a cluster, books under arms,
Bengali boys watch the waves before school.
Envy bubbles inside me.
I wish I could go to school, too.

"Life will be better in Bangladesh."
Mama had promised,
hope shining in her eyes.
Nani had said,
"You'll be able to walk to the market with friends."
Baba told us we'd be safer.
"Even to go to mosque," Nana had added.
"Bangladesh is full of Muslims.
We'll be free to practice our faith."

But in Burma, I learned at the madrasah
in a class just for girls.
In Burma, I had Nani and Nana,
who would make me special dried fish treats.
Nana had a way with spices,
he was the best cook, Nani always said.

Now I am left with a big hole,

right in the center of my chest.

Peering into its emptiness,

I wonder if school could fill it,

and reading and writing and books.

MY LONGING

"School's not important for girls," Baba insists.
His dark eyes meet mine.
It's easier to focus on the locks
rushing out from under his cap.
Yes, Baba, I understand.
My thoughts bounce back and forth inside my head.
I know what Baba will say next.

"You need to help feed our family."
I glance at the floor as Baba continues.
"If we could afford school,
we'd send your brother
because only boys
can change a family's fate."

His words squash me.
But, Baba, maybe girls can, too.
Maybe my hard work
my sweat
will bring our family

money

food

safety.

And if there's extra money,

couldn't I go to school?

SAMAJ

Back home in Maungdaw district,
we had samaj.
Here, there is no community
to share food with the hungrier families,
to help fix our roofs when they drip,
to keep peace when villagers argue,
to warn us of the burning.

Here, while I work, Mama takes care of our home.
There is no Hasina Auntie,
Mama's closest sister,
with her patient ways and high-pitched laugh
and big, round smiling face
to cheer us up.

Here, there are no family gatherings
after Friday night prayers,
with fried chicken, sticky rice, and banana leaf,
prepared by Nana,
served by Baba.

Here, we have just us.

THREE, PLEASE

I hear the adhan
and see men walking to mosque.
It must be past noon!
Wiggly lines of heat
sear the top of my head
through my double-folded orna.

Down the beach, I see girls
sellings chips, bread, jewelry, and shells.
There are no police today
walking around,
monitoring the area,
ready to run them off.

I wonder if they're all friends.
What are their names?
What do they dream of?
How do they keep cool?

My half-empty bucket
means half-empty bellies
means I must stay in this heat.

A couple sitting under a red umbrella
wave me over.
Hot sand crunches beneath my feet
as I walk their way.
I show them my eggs.
The lady smiles in approval,
her black sunglasses reflecting the water.
The man reaches for his wallet with one hand
and holds up three fingers with the other.

Tap-tap breaks the shell.
A quick swipe of each egg
against the string
attached to my bucket
reveals the yolk inside.
I sprinkle salt and red chili
on each open half.
My customers smile wide,
sinking their teeth into
a spicy snack
that tastes of the sea.

And just like that
my bucket
and heart
feel a little lighter.

SWAP

After his shift,
Khaled likes to talk with customers,
picking up English from tourists
and more Chittagonian from Bengalis.

Nani and Nana taught us Chittagonian.
They learned from trading
with Bengalis at the border.
Golden fiber bags were Nani's weak spot.
She swapped jade beads for them.
She swapped our words for theirs.

Some of them are the same
like *flower* and *three*,
and some are different
like *safe* and *rescue*.

More and more,
we must use their words
to get by,
to feel less on the
outside.

KEEPER

Like always,
Khaled has found his way.
He surfs with new friends
on a board he rents
with rasgulla instead of taka,
from a Bengali boy named Tariq.

Before the scraps from Khaled's café
make it to the rubbish
or to the dogs,
Khaled collects them,
bringing home roti or vegetable curry.
Even rasgulla.
Until Mama said more food
and less dessert.
Now the sweet, fluffy cheese balls
go to Tariq,
who has a sweet tooth
so big,
I see it when he laughs.

But the truth is

the boards are not really Tariq's.

Khaled says a missionary visiting Cox's Bazar

brought them.

The truth is

they are for all to share,

not for one to keep to themself.

The truth is

sometimes

hard to speak.

ZING-ZING

After three months,
my brother can catch waves
sometimes.
It doesn't matter to him
when he falls off
because each time he's out there,
he's having fun with his friends.
I hear them on the water.
Their splashing and laughing
could smother all the sadness in the world.

When Khaled sees me,
he comes in,
wet shirt stuck to his chest,
wavy hair glued to his forehead.

"What did you learn at the café today?" I ask.
"A lot," he replies.
I slap his hand away
as he reaches for an egg.
"Learning English is hard, too hard for you."
He pokes me,

and I sneer at him.
Though he is just teasing,
my throat tightens.
"I'm the best egg seller on the beach, Khaled!
If I can work, I can learn."

My brother splashes me,
and I let out a cry,
splashing him back.
My feet are in the water
sending a *zing-zing* charge
up my body.

Water can trick us.
It took my Nani and Nana
when we crossed into Bangladesh.
It draws more than a line on land.
It separates our old life
from our new life.

It wasn't always that way.
Auntie and Mama
brought me and Khaled
to bathe and swim in the river,
to jump and make big splashes.

Now, the water tries to whisk me away,
rushing around my feet,
burying them in sand.
It licks me *zing-zing* again,
my toes curl,
and suddenly I feel
courage.

"I'm going to ask Mama," I announce.
"Ask her what?" says Khaled.
"If I can go to school."

MY ANSWER

Mama's bun, free from her hijab,
wobbles as she speaks.
"Samira, girls don't need to go to school."

People think me and Mama
resemble each other.
We have eyes the color of charcoal,
eyebrows arched like bird wings.
Our round faces are mirrors,
except for the ring in Mama's nose.
Although she sits across the mat while we eat,
she suddenly seems so far away.

"Mama, but why not?"
Too late to swallow my words.
One look from her is enough.
Did you know eyes can be spiky?
I want to say, *Mama,*
I need something more
than just selling eggs.
Mama, before you sold
the gold necklace Baba gave you

to pay for these chickens,
before we came here,
before our Buddhist neighbors
said we didn't belong,
before the Burmese government
said Rohingya were from Bangladesh,
we had a life.
I had a life.

I stare at my dinner.
The pool of saltless dahl
looks sad.
Khaled makes silly slurps
to cheer me up,
but it doesn't work.
Like hot roti,
the conversation drops.

THE LESSON

While Mama and Baba still sleep,
Khaled taps my arm.
Why is he up so early?
He can teach me some English, he says.
I poke him. "Stop teasing, Khaled."
He grins and tells me to get up, poking me back.

Khaled acts like he's much older,
as if he learned everything about the world
in those twenty-four months he lived before me.
Though sometimes he is helpful
and kind,
he can be annoying!

He's not said his prayers this morning.
Did he forget
or has he chosen to delay
or skip them
just for me?
Either way, my lips are sealed.

"Let's get started," Khaled whispers
as he lays out the tools, treasures:
A small yellow pencil
with the letters *HB* on the side
and his notebook,
a gift from Nana,
crammed with
writing and pictures.

In a corner of our house,
the lesson begins.

Flicking past pages,
Khaled finds a blank space,
then writes fresh things.
"A, B, C," he whispers, pointing to the letters.
Their sounds tickle my ears like feathers,
and I smile.
I am learning English.
And, this morning,
I don't miss my cha!

OLD BAD DREAM

My day is not marked by the
rumbling of my tummy,
or the heat of the sun.
I don't even feel them because of
letters.

And now, lying awake at night,
I think about how proud Nani and Nana
would be of my learning,
if they were here,
if they hadn't gone
to the bottom of the river.

A tightness
squeezes my chest.
I imagine water
pushing against my limbs,
and below my feet,
nothing.
In a panic,
I kick hard
trying to swim to the surface.

But an anchor tied to my waist
keeps me down.

This vision appears often.
Each time, I'm back at the river crossing.
Our boat rocking back and forth,
inside, hungry babies crying,
parents clutching them to their chests,
wailing in fear
of losing their lives to water,
after dodging death
to get this far.

It happened so quickly.
Nani stood
to stretch her aching legs.
Nana helped.

And they slipped
over the side
of the boat.

Mama called out,
but it was too late.
Nani and Nana were slurped up
by milky brown chop.
Our outstretched hands

never met their grasp.
Their limbs weary,
their hearts long broken.
They had nothing left to hold.

Nani and Nana disappeared into the river,
vanishing forever.

WANDER

Me and Aisha watch the surf.
Aisha is my Rohingya friend,
seller of chips,
owner of two swaying ponytails.
She has crooked white teeth
that dazzle when she smiles.

We met on our hill
when I tripped on a rock.
A voice behind me
asked if I was hurt.
It was Aisha's.
She'd done the same thing,
she said.
Now, she's more careful.

Aisha came here a year before us
with only her
grandfather.
The rest of her family is a mystery
she never speaks of.

One day, she'll tell me about them,
she promises.
That moment
hasn't come,
but it feels close.

"See where the water
meets the sky?"
Her skinny finger points to the horizon.
"That's where I'm going one day."

"Where? That's the middle of the sea."
I don't want to imagine Aisha
on a boat.

"The whole world's out there, Samira.
There's Malaysia, Australia, America."
Aisha goes quiet,
like she's imagining all those places
from where we sit on a tuft of grass.

"Why'd you want to go to those places?
What's special about them?"
I've heard the names
but have never thought
of going.

Aisha turns
to look at me,
like my voice stopped
her daydream.

"Because every country is different.
Malaysia has towers so tall
the tops disappear into the clouds
on rainy days."

I throw my head back and squint,
trying to see that high up.

"Dada said the towers have eighty-eight floors."
Aisha says the number slowly.

"He's been there?"
I haven't met her grandfather yet,
but Aisha talks about him
all the time.
"No, a tourist on his old bus route told him,"
she explains, looking into the distance again.

Aisha is funny sometimes.
She likes to wander off
to distant places in her mind.

She's nothing like my best friend in Burma.
No one is like Sahara.

I gaze at the water.
A, B, C, D,
I repeat to myself each time the surf breaks.
A, B, C, D.
Tomorrow, I will learn more.

There's a tiny crack in the door,
and if I claw at it every day
with letters, sounds, then words,
the door will swing wide open,
and maybe behind it
there's a whole lot more.
That's the place I want to be.

NOSY EARS

"Take this and go to the market."
Mama hands Khaled some money.
"I need one small onion."
The market is my favorite!
I tuck my hair into my orna,
the dark blue one,
a birthday gift from Sahara.
"Ok, you can go as well."
Mama reads my mind.

As we approach,
we're embraced by beeping tom toms,
Bangla music blaring from radios,
loud chatter of customers,
and the calls of sellers
tempting passers-by,
their goods lit up
by bare bulbs swinging
in the breeze.

Cloth sacks bulging with
masoor dahl

and mung beans
rest lopsided on shelves.
What could I cook with them?
Something with a dash of spices
from jars filled with
earth brown,
fiery red,
and ivory white.
Nana would know which ones to add.

Across the street is the fabric shop,
where bundles of silk
sparkle.
I see lime-green saris
with copper borders,
ink-blue saris
with silver embroidery.
Red velvet boxes boast of
golden bangles and earrings.

But the most tempting are the sweet treats!
Mountain-high squiggles
of sticky chanar jilapi,
huge silver vats brimming
with milky rasmalai.

The mix of sweet and savory
swirling in the air
fills my nostrils and belly.

Me and Khaled come to a vegetable stand
where two Bengali women talk,
and my nosy ears catch words
I cannot unhear.

"More Rohingya have been coming.
But how many more can we take?"
one whispers.
"They get more than us.
Food, water, housing in the camp.
Some even work.
What about the jobs our families need?"

Her friend nods in agreement.
"The camp is overcrowded," she replies.
"Surely they can't stay here much longer?
Burma doesn't want them.
Who says we do?"

I want them!
If Auntie and Sahara come,
they can live with us!
They won't take up extra room

or jobs

or water

or food.

We'll share

everything.

SURPRISE

Cha in belly,
eggs in bucket,
I'm ready for work.
Cluck, cluck, our chickens say goodbye.
When every day starts the same,
I feel safe, and I like that.
I think it eases Mama, too.

Leaving the house
means risking a lot.
Some Bengalis harass us
and threaten to tell the police
we are living
moving
working
outside the camp.

"I'll be careful, Mama."
I smile, and her brow relaxes
a little.

Aisha sits in the shade of the trees
at the beach,
two buckets next to her.
I peek into one and spot shells,
some smooth and shiny with dark brown flecks,
others spirals of green coiled tight,
or spiky and bumpy,
the color of coconut milk.

The other bucket has jewelry.
Gold earrings and bracelets
with shells and sparkly gems
arranged in neat rows
poked through holes
on pieces of cardboard.

"Pssst, hey, Aisha."
A girl in a faded pink and purple shalwar kameez
appears from behind a thick tree trunk.
She's short and stocky
and wears a side ponytail.
In one hand she holds a bucket.
Tucked under the other arm
is a white surfboard.
Aisha reaches up to the sky,
as if she's stretching.

"That's our secret code,"
Aisha whispers.
"It means no police are here
to run us off for selling."

The girl comes out from hiding.
"Maya, this is Samira," says Aisha.
"She's new to Cox's Bazar
and doesn't have friends."

Aisha can say strange things sometimes.
She doesn't mean to.
I've learned
it's just her way.

Maya smiles at me,
and when she does,
her round button nose wrinkles.
"I've seen you at the beach before.
Where are you from?
What's in your bucket?
Can you surf?"
Questions tumble from Maya,
one after the other.
She pauses.
I begin, "Hi, I'm from—"

But Maya launches
into another flow.
Chittagonian is hard for me to understand
when spoken so quickly.

Aisha seems to have no problem.
"Yes," she replies slowly,
"the waves look good today.
I'll be here to watch
over the buckets."

On hearing her words,
Maya places her bucket full of bread
next to the others
and rushes to the water
with her board.
"Nice to meet you, Samira,"
she calls out as she goes.

I watch her join the other surfers,
and I think of my friends in Burma
and the things we'd do together,
like picking padauk flowers
hanging on low branches.
Sahara, a head taller than me,
could reach up high

and collect even more.
I think she liked that I was shorter.

Leaving Aisha in the lookout spot,
I walk into the wet sand,
letting my toes sink in
and cool water ripple over them.

Like birds riding the wind,
Maya and her friends
glide across the waves.

I can't stop staring
because I want this moment
to last.
I want to be as happy
and free
as these girls
on waves.

KNIVES AND CLUBS

Aisha pulls a bag of chips
from the torn pocket of her dress.
"Hungry?" she asks.
She rips it open before I say yes.
Our walk to the lake
is crunchy and salty and
delicious.

"I hope Rubi remembers
to bring her needle and thread.
See this?"
Aisha points to the pocket.
"She promised to fix it for a bag of chips."

"I could never sew," I admit.
"Needles can prick your finger,
and seeing blood makes me dizzy."
Though it shouldn't.
Back home
I'd seen more blood than most
from men armed with knives and clubs
and lies.

Men who were once our friendly
Buddhist neighbors.

Aisha nods.
She knows what I'm talking about.
"A stolen cart,
a broken store window,
they'd blame us for anything," she tells me.
"Dada always pointed to the back door
when we heard loud voices.
That meant hide behind a bus.
It was our code."

"The bus your dada drove?"
I ask Aisha.
This is the first time
she's invited me into her
old life.

"Yes, our apartment in Yangon
was near the bus station,
where Baba and Dada were drivers.
Me, Mama, and Dadi,
we'd step out the back to hide
behind a parked bus.
It's a good hiding spot."

They lived in the city?
Her baba was a driver, too?
There's a lot I don't know
about my friend.
But I do know
when she clears her throat
and changes the subject,
it's time to drop the questions.

Our walk to the lake
is more than a walk.
It's a pocket of time
and space
to share little bits of ourselves
with each other.

MEETING

We finish our chips as we arrive
at a body of muddy water
lined with pine trees at one end.
Maya waves from across the lake,
her face bright and cheery.
I didn't recognize her at first,
her hair is not in a ponytail
but drapes over one shoulder.
"Over here," she calls,
pinching her nose
with her finger and thumb.
"That side stinks."
She points to a pile of
festering rubbish.

We walk around,
and while I stop at the edge,
Aisha wades in,
her loose pants clinging to her legs,
water up to her knees.

"I'm glad you both made it."
Maya floats
beside two other girls.

"Samira's a little afraid of the water."
This is not the way
I want to be introduced.
Aisha realizes,
her cheeks flush,
and she quickly says,
"This is Tariq's sister, Nadia."
Her chin jerks in the direction of a girl
with slim long limbs stretching out before her
and a thick braid that floats behind.

"You don't like water?" the girl asks.
She faces the trees
and rather than turning around,
she throws a quick glance back.
"Are you scared it'll bite?"
She snickers at her own remark,
and Maya and the other girl
laugh after a short delay.
It takes me a few seconds to understand.
I smile awkwardly
when I get it.

I'm not ready to go in the water.
I don't know these girls,
and I don't feel
like explaining why.

"And this is Rubi," says Aisha,
interrupting my thoughts.
A girl with thick, short hair
and an oval face spits out water.
"Eww!" Maya shrieks.
"It was an accident!" the girl yells.
She smiles at me, then adds,
"It's shallow, so you don't have to be scared.
Nadia has lifesaving skills.
You'll help, right, Nadia?"

Nadia twists the end of her braid
and says nothing.
Aisha translates for me,
and I look down at my feet.
I don't need help
understanding.
Naida's reaction tells me everything.

"Oh, I can swim," I say, trying
to ease the awkwardness.

"It's just been some time."
I wonder if I sound
like I'm making it up,
and then Aisha gives me
the chance to prove it.
"Come on, Samira," she insists.
"Just try."

I'd rather be a gecko
so I could scamper off
and hide behind a rock.
But to show these girls
I can do it,
that I'm not lying,
I brace myself
and let my toes get wet.
Then I wade in,
feeling water swish around my legs
and my feet sink into dirt.

With each step,
I feel less outside.
With each step,
I show them and myself
I can do it.
And the whole time,

I'm whispering inside,
This is not the river we crossed,
this is not the river we crossed.

Just as I reach the group,
Nadia says, "It's time for us to go."
She stands up,
clothes dripping,
and Maya and Rubi
follow her.

I elbow Aisha,
and pretend to sew
with my thumb and finger.
"Oh, yes, I forgot!" she says.
"Rubi, can you fix my pocket?"
Rubi opens her mouth to speak,
but Nadia answers.
"Maybe tomorrow, Aisha.
She doesn't have the time right now."
Nadia wrings her braid
and starts to walk off.

Rubi gives Aisha a sorry smile,
then follows Nadia.
Maya waves goodbye
and joins them.

Me and Aisha are left
standing in the lake.
I wonder if she also has
a bitter taste in her mouth.

BELONGING

Being ignored
and left out
turns everything upside down
so you're swirling,
not knowing,
not trusting which way is up.

I've learned that belonging,
having a home,
having a country,
means everything,
is everything.

Our country, our home, is Burma.
Not Myanmar, like the government
calls it.
Our beloved Burma.
Nani and Nana once said
farming has run through the veins
of Rohingya people
since time began.
It gave life to my village.

My family's land,
dotted with red chili plants,
lined with rice paddies,
was what we knew,
what we loved.
We ate all we needed
and sold the rest at the market.

Nani and Nana told family stories.
Our history passed down
by word of mouth.
But Nana told Khaled to write it down
in his notebook.
And he did.

Our grandparents' parents
told stories
of how Rohingya lived with Buddhists
when the British took control of Burma.
During WWII
we sided with the British,
but Buddhists sided with the Japanese.
When the British rule ended
and Burma became independent,
we thought we'd be given
our own Muslim state.

That day never came.
Instead, we lost our rights.
The Burmese government said
we don't belong in Burma,
we never did,
we're from Bangladesh
and should go back.

And these lies,
this poison,
spread to the military and police
and through towns and villages
until our Buddhist neighbors
believed them.

But different people come from our country,
like Mon, Karen, Chin.
And Rohingya.

That's why Auntie stayed.
"It is our homeland," she said,
and she wouldn't be told otherwise.

BURNING VILLAGES

Slowly, children's laughter was muffled
by the stomping of soldiers' boots
and calls for
no more mosques
no markets
no samaj.
These rules, tight,
gripping our necks,
were meant to wipe us out.
Our culture.
Our people.

Our Rohingya neighbors disappeared
without a trace.
The crops in our fields,
left shriveled and crumbling,
were eaten by no one.
We weren't free to tend to them.
We couldn't even fetch water from the wells.

Should we go before it gets worse?
Mama and Baba began to whisper.

No, *we stay*, Nani and Nana whispered back.

This is our home.

You know what happened to those

who fled to a camp in Bangladesh.

They were forced back,

back to nothing,

back to homes reduced to cinder.

Though staying and going

both scared me,

I wish I had begged everyone

to come with us.

My whole family and Sahara's.

But leaving also means taking risks,

like my Nani and Nana.

Now we live with that risk

we can never take back.

A NEW GAME

With no Nana around,
Khaled gets bored.
They spent time together,
sometimes just walking,
sometimes just talking.
Nana taught Khaled boli khela.
I'd watch them and laugh because
wrestling is funny.
It turns you and your rival
into a ball of sweaty limbs,
twisting and grappling.

Now, Khaled plays a new game,
especially when there's no surf.
He holds his bat up.
"Mama, can I go?"
Cricket is king here.
My brother loves it!

Swish-swish,
Mama sweeps the kitchen
with her grass broom.

She nods in approval.
Khaled plays with Rohingya boys
who leave the main camp.
Baba says they're called registered refugees
and have papers to prove it.
We are called unregistered
because we live outside
the camp.
It was already overflowing
with families when we arrived.

We must be careful, Baba always warns.
Even when we just go out for cricket.

When I ask if I can join Khaled,
Mama's back goes rigid.
A few seconds pass.
"Be home by sunset."
Sometimes Mama is heaven!
And just like that,
I am free
to watch cricket.

GLOW

The boys wait by the coconut palms
at the bottom of the hill.
Excitement ripples through them
when they see Khaled coming.
Back home, Baba was popular, too.
People came to him for advice,
to sip cha,
to talk about their day,
their troubles.

That Baba is different from today's Baba.
The Baba who comes up the hill now
stoops forward,
holding his lower back,
his face a grimace.

Shrimping is hard work.
Baba never complains,
but we know.
When he sees us, he waves us on
and continues home.

In the distance,
Bengali boys walk toward us.
Someone yells,
"Hey, what're you doing?
You think you can play cricket here?"

One of the boys is
Tariq.
When he sees Khaled,
he gives him a quick nod
and tells his friends,
"It's ok, these guys can play."
Then he calls out, "We'll go against you.
Let's see how good you are."
Does this mean Khaled owes him two
portions of rasgulla now?

From a spot under the trees,
I watch
feet running fast
an arm swinging
a shiny red ball flying.
Tariq grips the rough, splintery stick.
Thwack! He makes contact.
The ball rockets skyward,
above an explosion of racing boys.
"You're the fastest runner!"

The boys applaud.

"And the most fearless."

Tariq's face glows.

And I imagine

when he eats dessert,

he looks just as happy.

GETTING ACQUAINTED

I hear a holler
coming from the beach path
and turn to see Maya,
walking along,
swinging an empty bucket.

She runs across the dirt
and ducks to avoid the ball
and complaints from players.
Maya gleefully claims a seat
next to me in the shade.
I wonder,
if Nadia was with her,
would they sit across from me instead?

"You like cricket, Samira?" she asks.
I tell her I'm watching Khaled learn.
"Tariq is the best at cricket,
and he loves it when we cheer for him."
I like Maya and her questions and her nose that wrinkles
when she smiles.

"There's no surf today?" I ask,
hoping my Chittagonian sounds good.
Maya doesn't give me a strange look,
and I'm relieved.
"We only get to use the surfboards
when Nadia's around
and only for an hour," she explains.
"If Tariq wasn't her brother,
we'd never be able to use them."
Maya tells me more about
Tariq and the surfboards,
and even though I already know a little,
I learn a whole lot more
about him.
I look at Maya and wonder how someone
so small can hold so much knowing.
"A few years ago," she says,
"Tariq learned surfing
from a visitor
who arranged for boards to be sent over.
'Invite your friends,
and we can all surf together,' he'd said.
But as soon as he left Cox's Bazar,
Tariq took the boards to his house
behind the market
where he stores them.
He hands out business cards

to tourists with information
about board rentals."

Before I get to ask another question,
Maya waves at Rubi, who
sets down her bucket
and shakes out her hand
to release the tension.
She cracks her knuckles,
then picks up her bucket again.

"Did you sell much today?"
Rubi kneels by Maya.
"Not really," she replies,
pointing to her full bucket.
"But Nadia sold all her jewelry
and went home.
I wish I could sew clothes instead, like Mama.
The money's better,
and you don't have to carry
a heavy bucket."

Maya flexes her forearm.
"It's good training for surfing.
I can carry your bucket for you
sometime, Rubi.
It'll help build up these muscles."

Turning to me, she asks,
"Have you ever tried it?
You said you can swim.
Because if you can't, it's fine,
you can still surf.
It's just scary when you fall off.
You have to hold on to the board."

"Like this."
Rubi rolls onto her behind
and thrashes her arms and legs
to make us laugh.

But the next minute,
we are distracted by a loud *thwack!*

Khaled hits the ball.
Maya squeals in celebration,
then inhales sharply
when she realizes Tariq is not the batsman.
The ball shoots over the trees
and out of sight.

I agree with Baba,
our Khaled will bring
something good.
He'll change the fate of our family.

WHAT'S IT LIKE?

Walking back up our hill, I ask,
"What's it like to not be scared?"
Khaled throws me a sideways glance
as he wipes sweat from his cheeks
with the back of his hand.
"I mean of the water and surfing."

My brother's answer is full of certainty.
"Surfing doesn't scare me.
How can you be afraid of something
when you haven't even tried it?"

Everything is clear for Khaled.
For me, everything is the sky smudged gray-black
before monsoon rains let loose.

RADIO NEWS

On Saturday afternoons,
Khaled and Baba often go to a tea shop.
For a handful of shrimp,
the owner lets them
tune into a radio show.

They bring back news
that sometimes makes us go silent,
like when we learned Rohingya are not allowed
to go to the doctor
or buy food from the market
back home.

Other times, there is no news
because foreign reporters are banned
from going into Rakhine
to see villages like ours.
As months pass,
our fear of being forgotten
by the rest of the world
grows.

RIPTIDE

From where I sit on the beach,
I see Rubi's head bobbing above the water.
She twists and turns,
her arms flailing
until she finds it.
Her board.
It's for surfing
and for keeping her afloat
because without it,
she'd drown.

I set my bucket down
on an uncrowded section of beach,
wondering if
Rubi's ok,
if I should help.

She drifts farther out
and down the coast
until the tide finally washes her in
to safety.

Rubi walks back up slowly,
as if her legs are cement posts.
"The rip . . ." she says, breathless.
"It just pulls you out to sea
like it's a giant octopus."
She lets her board slip onto the sand
and bends over,
resting her hands on her knees.

"You know, if you kick harder
with your legs," I say,
"and lean forward more,
it can help you swim.
And when there's a rip . . ."

Rubi frowns.
"I didn't ask for help.
I've never even seen you swim,
because maybe you can't!"
Before she's recovered,
Rubi picks up her board
and rushes into the water.

"I didn't mean . . ."
But I'm too late.
A tip, some friendly advice
to help save energy,

that's all I was offering.

The sound of breaking waves

drowns my words.

And I'm left standing on the beach,

feeling foolish

and misunderstood.

FATE CHANGER

Happy, cheerful voices
come from our house.
I open the door to see
Baba patting Khaled on the back
and Mama pouring extra dahl into her pot.
"Let's celebrate," she says,
joy flashing in her eyes.

I set down my empty bucket.
"What's going on? What's the news?"
Khaled explains, and with each word,
his grin turns into a broad smile.

Mr. Ali is impressed with Khaled's work
and how he talks to his customers.
The aid workers have even asked him
to translate Rohingya into English.

Khaled leans in.
When no one was around,
Mr. Ali slipped a folded
Tk.10 note

into his hand
because the aid workers stay longer,
and they bring friends
who spend money at the café.
Now Mr. Ali says Khaled is
his best employee!

As Mama prepares dahl and rice for dinner,
she hums.
Baba tends to loose lashings around the house.
Khaled smiles as he writes in his notebook.
He turns it this way and that
like he always does
when he's drawing pictures,
and I watch my brother and think
how clever he is!

LESSON #11

Me and Khaled forget
our cramped home
as we sit together outside.
I thank God for this cozy new spot
for learning,
where we are crowned by
clear blue skies
and cloaked by
tall green grass.

Huddled here is being back in Burma.
After fetching garlic for Mama
from the vegetable stand,
me and Sahara would hide in the trees
or run along riverbanks,
rice paddies lining one side,
green hills hugging the other.

Khaled nudges me.
I snap out of my daydream
and repeat the words.

My brother listens,
stopping me, correcting me.
Sometimes he's so strict,
he could even be a real teacher.
But he gives me a smile every time
I say a word right,
and I offer him a secret egg in return.

So far, we've had eleven lessons,
the same number as my age.
And I've also found out
English has rules
and patterns
like cat, hat, sat.

But the best discovery:
I learn quickly.
If Sahara were here, she'd tell me,
You've always been good at schoolwork,
remember when in madrasah
you recited the lines
we'd just read.
This would not surprise her.
But she might be struck
by Bengali girls
going out without hijabs.

And me
in shalwar kameez
instead of a thaami.

All these new things
make my chest flutter
like I'm a bird ready for flight.
Now, each moment of learning
makes anything feel possible,
makes the world seem smaller
so one day
I could even fly over it.

READY

"Psst!" I whisper.
Barely awake, Khaled groans,
"What do you want, Samira?
It's too early to read."
He turns his back to me.

I throw off my sheet
and squat down close to him.
"I want to go down to the beach and swim.
Come watch over me,
in case I need help.
I'll feel better if someone is there."
Khaled sits up and rubs his eyes.
"Why? What's gotten into you?"

I can think of a few answers.
To show Rubi
to prove to myself
to make friends with water again.
But my words to Khaled are simple.

"I'm ready."

My brother gives me a big smile.

"What are we waiting for?"

SAFE SEABED

Our feet make
the first prints
on the sand.
Khaled dives into the sea.
Stroke, kick, stroke, kick.

Cool choppy water licks my waist.
Underneath my feet,
a bumpy, poky seabed.
Its roughness feels right,
it tells me I am safe.
Where it's shallow,
I bend my knees,
make circles with my arms,
and lean forward.
Khaled watches me close by,
his arm outstretched,
in case I need help.

Lips sucked in, sharp inhale,
I launch myself,
and a *zing-zing*

rushes over my whole body.
I make a few strokes
and swim toward Khaled.
He cheers and splashes me,
and I splash him back.
Showing off my best stroke,
I swim away.
Khaled follows.

We go back and forth
in a cat-and-mouse chase
that I didn't know I'd missed.

MY STUDENT

Five surfers rise and fall
over the rolling sea.
I know two of them.
Nadia's board cuts through
small, bumpy waves.
She stands like bamboo,
sturdy but flexible,
arms out by her side,
her ripped sleeve
flapping in the wind.

Maya wobbles,
her orna hangs limp
around her neck.
She steps back,
loses her balance,
and makes a big splash
as she hits the water.

Next, they come in.
Maya asks, "Been watching for long?"

She gives me an embarrassed smile.
"That wasn't my best wave.
I can do much better."

"I just got here," I say,
getting up to my feet.
"The water looks refreshing.
I can't wait to jump in."

"Come on," Nadia says to Maya.
She wipes water drops from her face.
"Tariq wants the boards back,
and my mother's expecting me home."
She tips her chin my way,
which I think means goodbye,
and starts to walk off.
Maya hesitates for a few seconds, rooted,
then finally speaks up.
"Wait, can I keep mine
for a little while?"
Nadia stops in her tracks.

Maya gives her a sideways glance,
as if she's afraid of the response.
"I want to practice a little more," she explains.

Nadia chews on her lip
and blinks rapidly
as if she was caught off guard.

I'm wondering if Maya and Rubi
ever get to use the boards
without Nadia.
Is it safe, when they
can't swim?

"Well, you know how dangerous it is.
Kids have drowned out there,"
Nadia warns.

Maya nods and gives her a weak smile.
"I'll be careful," she says.
"And Samira knows how to swim,
if I need help.
As soon as I'm done
I'll take the board back.
I promise."

Nadia gives Maya a smirk.
"I guess you'll find out if Samira can swim."
Then she finally says,
"Ok, I'll tell Tariq to expect you later,
but don't be too tardy."

Maya's eyes sparkle.
She grins
and thanks Nadia
twice.

With Nadia in the distance,
Maya loses no time.
"Will you teach me to swim?"

Saying it out loud gives her more confidence.
"There's no one else to teach me
apart from Nadia,
but she always
makes an excuse."

"Like she doesn't really want to,
you mean?"
Maya's cheeks flush.
I know Rubi also needs to learn.
Every time she goes out to surf,
she takes a risk.
If Nadia is the only one
who can swim
and save lives in this group,
what can they do without her?

I look back into the woods
and both ways down the beach
to see if the coast is clear.
"How about now?"
When Maya hears my words,
she does a little jiggle.
Then she coils her hair
into a tight bun
and wraps a tie around it.
She's ready to learn.

For the next hour,
I show Maya how to kick hard
and use her hands
like spoons, not forks.

I stay close,
balancing across her surfboard.
Maya feels better
knowing it's right there.
She can reach out any time
she wants help, she says.

With my belly on its hard surface
and my legs dangling in the sea,
I am struck by how easily
the board moves on the water.

Smooth,

no resistance

free.

It wants to go.

It can take you to any place,

and I like that.

"Samira! Samira. I can swim, watch me."

Maya makes a few strokes,

and when she reaches me,

she props her belly on the board,

coughing from water she swallowed.

We celebrate her new skill

with a storm of kicking.

Maya's splashes go

high in the air.

She's got strong legs,

a lot stronger than mine.

But Maya's smile suddenly vanishes.

A woman walks along the beach,

hands on her hips.

"What are you doing?

I told you no surfing."

She wears a menacing look

and stops as close as possible

to where we float.

"You don't even know how to swim.
You'll drown.
Did you think about
the shame
you'll bring to our family?"

Maya quickly grabs her board
and steps out of the water.
"Mama, I know you told me, I'm sorry.
But I can . . ."
Her voice trails off
when her mother grabs her hair.
Maya pulls free and runs away.
Her mother walks quickly,
trying to catch up.

I dash into the woods, where I crouch low
and wring my wet hair and clothes.

Now that I'm older,
I'm not supposed to swim,
according to my faith.
If Mama and Baba were here,
I'd be in big trouble, too.
Thinking about it makes me shiver,
and the shiver follows me into bed,
as I lay on my sleeping mat at night.

DADA

Aisha's house is high up on the hill.
Its walls are like ours,
but the roof is a sheet of tin,
the kind that makes
a deafening sound
in the rain.

Inside, her dada sits cross-legged.
"Come in, Samira."
White teeth,
like Aisha's,
shine when he smiles.

The gravel in his voice,
the rivers of veins merging
on the backs of his hands,
and his thick, stubby toes
remind me of Nana.
My whole body
melts in his presence
so much,
I feel myself coming apart.

But I hold back my tears.
Thanking him for Khaled's pants
is a good distraction.
Her dada said he got them
from an aid worker.
And even though he finds his longyi
more comfortable,
he says he likes the freedom of choice
he did not have in Burma.

And her dada talks nonstop.
I'm not sure if it's to me or
at me,
but I don't care,
because my heart is open,
drinking in the sound
of his voice.

He drove visitors to sights
in Yangon
to Buddhist temples
golden pagodas
and night markets.
And the tourists he met
from China, Thailand, and France
shared stories with him
of their homelands.

Now I know why
when Aisha talks of other countries
it's like she's sharing her own
memories.

Aisha picks up her bucket,
and her dada tells us to
look out for each other.
He worries,
just like my family,
about police chasing us off,
about being reported for working on the beach,
about the dogs stealing our food.

As we walk to work,
Aisha tells me more.
"Our apartment had maps
pinned to the walls," she says.
"I memorized each name Dada told me.
I thought, 'When I grow up,
I'll go to those cities
with Dada.'"
Her eyes glaze over,
and it reminds me of how I felt
when I lay on Maya's board,
bold and free.

"Have you ever tried surfing?" I ask.
Aisha shakes her head.
"Who will take care of Dada
if something ever happened
to me?"

And her question makes me wonder,
is it a good time to ask?
I've told her
about Nani and Nana,
after all.
Or is it too painful for her
to talk about her family?
Before I know it,
my curiosity
gets the better of me.
"Where's the rest of your family?
You never talk about them."

Aisha stares at the path ahead.
It narrows and swings to the left
before opening up to the lake.
And with a gentle smile
across her face,
Aisha points upward to the sky.
I instantly know what she means,
and this gesture,

this understanding,
brings us closer
without
another word.

INGREDIENTS

"You're a better swimmer than me!"
I say over the lake
as I watch Maya
kick her legs
and move her arms.
She wears a serious expression,
like she's focusing hard.
"Not really, but thanks, Samira."

Rubi sits next to Aisha,
sewing her ripped pocket.
"Better than me, right?"
I know Rubi's talking about the other day,
when I offered her advice.

Her gaze stays with the needle
as she pushes it through the fabric.
"Keep still, Aisha!"
Aisha freezes.
"Anyway, my parents would be mad
if they knew I was in the water
almost every day," Rubi adds.

She makes a shivering motion,
as if imagining their reaction.
"I tell Mama a surfboard
can save your life,
and she says so does keeping
off the water!"

Rubi puts on a voice,
to imitate her mother.
We giggle and relax a little.

"At least your parents
don't chase you down the beach!" cries Maya.
She steps out of the lake
and squeezes the ends of her shalwar.
Then she tells Rubi and Aisha
about what happened.
"And Mama worries
everyone will talk about me
or I'll be swept out to sea."

"Maybe they're talking about you
being a stylish surfer," Rubi jokes.
She holds her hands out by her side
and sways from side to side,
like she's riding a wave.
Rubi is quite the actress

with the way she moves
and her different voices.
She loves to make an audience laugh.

"What's so funny?" someone calls out
from the other side of the lake.
Nadia walks over quickly.
"Mama and Baba insisted
I stay at home this morning.
I had to sweep the floor and
fetch water
while my brother slept
and went to visit his friends."
She lets out a sigh.
"What did I miss?"

Rubi pats the ground,
and Nadia takes the invitation.
"It's as good as new," Rubi brags.
She snips the end of the thread
and packs the needle and scissors
into a small paper bag.

Aisha admires her dress,
digging her hand in
to test the stitching.
"You're lucky your mom sews."

She gives a bag of chips to Rubi,
who takes a handful
and passes the bag to Maya.
Maya takes three chips,
puts one on top of the other,
and bites down on the stack.

"Mama has always sewn," Rubi replies.
"And her mother.
I've been thinking about
sewing little cloth bags
for my shells
so I can make more money."

Maya approves. "That's a really good idea."
She offers me the chip bag,
and I take it
and read the English words
on the back.
"*Po-ta-to,*" I say.
"Huh?" Aisha shrugs.
I point to the list of ingredients.
"That's what we're eating."
Aisha examines the packet,
then gapes at me.
"How do you know, Samira?"
"Read more!" Maya cries.

Fat! Salt! Po-ta-to!
After I say each ingredient,
Aisha copies me.
Maya and Rubi repeat the words, too.
Rubi's accent is good.

The only person who
doesn't join in
is Nadia.
She picks at her fingernails,
and with each word, I feel
the wall between us
grow higher.

SHAKING

After my morning cha,
Mama plants a kiss on my cheek.
"I'm leaving early to sell eggs," I tell her.

Stopping in the woods,
I inhale the salty air
and close my eyes.
Reading and swimming
bring joy and pleasure
to my long day.
What would I do without them?

The sudden sound of voices
coming from the beach
catches my attention.
I squat in case it's Maya's mother.
She knows my face now
and might be looking for me.
Or it could be the police.
But when I study the area,
I don't see Maya's mother
nor anyone in a navy-blue uniform.

Instead, I see Nadia and Rubi
sitting on the sand.
I hear my name as they talk,
so I crouch back down
and listen for a moment.
I haven't figured out Rubi yet,
and Nadia is never friendly to me.
I decide to listen in.

The distant *vroom-vroom*
of a tom tom engine
means I only catch one word.
It's "dog."

Is Rubi calling
me
a dog?

That's what the soldiers called us
when they stormed our village
and yelled at us to get out
because we were nothing but
dogs from Bangladesh!

My heart races,
and I break out into a sweat.

Nadia laughs out loud.
She thinks what Rubi says is funny?

I watch as Nadia stands up,
shakes the sand off her kameez,
and arranges her braid.
Rubi grabs their buckets,
and they both walk toward
early-morning beachgoers,
still laughing.

I clamp my hand
down on my mouth
to stop myself from
shouting at them.

The comfort of Mama's kiss
this morning,
the thrill of thinking
about the new things I am doing
are gone.
Even though I wish
I hadn't come to the beach early,
at least I learned
what this Rubi girl
is all about.

ALL OVER AGAIN

"You're quiet tonight, Samira."
Baba looks from me to Khaled
as we eat dinner.
"Has your brother been teasing you again?"
If Baba knew what Rubi said,
he'd be bubbling with rage, too.

"Just tired?" Mama's hand touches mine,
and I force a smile,
holding back my tears.

This feeling is not new.
Back home, when villagers started
the rumors about us,
I had this same tight feeling
in my throat,
and it hurts.

Words flicker in front of me
as I lie on my sleeping mat.
"Rohingya are burning their own villages."
"Women and children are being slayed by Rohingya."

These lies were spread in person
and online.
Facebook had stories that weren't true,
photos that were fake.

They believe lies?
Nani had said when we told her,
an edge to her voice I seldom heard.
That's dangerous. No wonder
our Buddhist neighbors have turned on us!
That same anger boils in me now.

Tomorrow, I won't be quiet.
Tomorrow, I'll speak
to Rubi.

SPEAK

I set my bucket down on the sand
and plant myself next to Aisha.
"There you are," she says.
"I was wondering where you were."

Nadia sits cross-legged by her side,
playing with the flap
of her torn kameez.

Rubi kneels behind Maya,
braiding her hair,
and when she smiles at me,
my stomach clenches.

I thought I was ready.
I had practiced
what to say
and how to say it.
Now the words get stuck.

"Rubi can do your hair next." Maya smiles.
"I like wearing my hair different ways," she says.

"It's fun."

I don't want Rubi's hands

on me.

It's hard enough

just sitting

on the same beach as her.

"Is something wrong?" Nadia asks.

I'm close to shouting out,

Everything's wrong!

Rubi was unkind,

and you didn't defend me

when she called me a dog.

You just laughed.

I guess that's no big surprise,

coming from Nadia.

Maya cranes her neck

to see me better.

"What happened, Samira?

You look so sad.

Tell us.

You don't have to have a braid."

Maya, please hush!

"Ask Rubi," I finally snap.
"She can tell you."

Rubi drops a section of braid.
"Huh? What do you mean?"

Now I am ready.
The words flow, and I tell them everything I heard and saw.

Aisha glowers at Rubi.
"Is that true?
Did you say that?"
Rubi's mouth drops open,
but I answer for her.
"Yes, she did.
And she meant it."

"Wait, Samira."
Nadia gives me a piercing look.
"You misunderstood.
She didn't say that."

Rubi shakes her head quickly.
"N-n-no," she stammers,
"I didn't call you a dog.
There was one on the beach,

and I pointed it out to Nadia.
It was chasing a red crab,
and the crab turned to
pinch the dog's nose,
and then it ran away."

I go over the scene in my mind.
It's true—there are always dogs around.
But I only remember
the tom tom's loud engine.
Did I really mishear her words?

Rubi leaves Maya's half-done hair
and drops to her knees in front of me.
"I would never think that!"
Her voice wavers.
"I didn't call you anything."
She grabs my hands
and squeezes gently.

"I know you're angry at me," I explain.
"For telling you how to swim,
but to call me a . . ."
I refuse to repeat her word.
"Swimming? Oh, that?" she says,
"I was just frustrated that time.

At myself.

But I promise,

I've never said an unkind word

about you."

The tender look on Rubi's face

and the warmth in her hands

make me think

maybe she is telling the truth

after all.

Even though a weight

lifts from my heart,

I'm still a little

confused and embarrassed,

but mostly, I'm feeling

so tired and weary

from the rage.

AN UPDATE

Mr. Ali said Khaled can bring me,
Mama, and Baba to the café
to watch the news on TV.
Mama didn't even make cha this morning,
but we don't mind.

We huddle on the floor
in the most beautiful kitchen I've seen,
with sinks big enough to fit giant pots,
shelves full of oil cans, rice, pulses,
spices, herbs, onions, and garlic.

"Nana would love to cook
in this kitchen!" I say.
"Shh!" Khaled turns up the volume
as the report begins.

A neat-bearded newscaster,
his crisp business suit,
and set of straight teeth,
appear on the screen.
At first, he talks about local news

and then we hear the word *Rohingya.*

We all lean in.

"The Burmese and Bangladeshi governments say

the violence has decreased," he reports.

"But fleeing refugees claim

arrests and arson attacks

aimed at driving out the Rohingya

continue."

Mama rocks back and forth

as she listens.

The reporter finishes with words

that feel

like a blow.

"Bangladeshi authorities have refused

to accept the refugees

and have pushed back

boatloads of Rohingya."

Mama covers her eyes

with her hands,

as if she expects to see a picture

of those boats.

Baba remains silent,

jaw twitching

as he grinds his teeth.

Mr. Ali stands in the back
until the report ends.
When we turn off the TV,
he comes to us.

"It's not easy," he says.
"Turning back your people
may sound cruel,
but food and water are already
scarce here.
Since the camps opened,
it costs more to see a doctor.
A tom tom ride used to be Tk.30,
now it's double.
People are worried
for the future of our town."

"As soon as we have our rights back,
we'll go home," Baba responds.
"And I pray that day will come soon.
For now, we have nowhere else to go."

Silence
fills the space
between us.

Mr. Ali pats Khaled's back
and smiles weakly.
He invites us
to watch TV another time.

We leave with a report
that will be hard to share
with neighbors
who hope for good news.
But I refuse to wish
for anything less
than our basic rights
because if I do,
my heart will stop
beating.

PUNCHES

The plastic bucket in
these hands
will go down this hill twice
because today
I'm selling double
the amount of eggs.

There are lots of tourists
renting out red umbrellas and chairs,
strolling along the shore,
splashing kids in shallow water.
They sit in innertubes
bobbing up and down in the water,
even riding waves.

On a gust of wind,
the smell of spicy meat
from a kebab seller
drifts my way.
Next to him, a group of boys
are busy people-watching.
Tariq is amongst them,

and when he catches my eye,
he leans in to his friends,
as though he's whispering.
"Go back where you belong!"
One of them calls out.
Was it Tariq or another boy?
I don't know for sure,
but his words are like
punches to my body.
I tell myself,
Just keep walking
just keep
just.

But my anger is too hot to hold,
so I shout, "Leave me alone!"

When Khaled sees my seething,
he runs across the beach.
"Samira, come this way."
He wipes my tears with his fingertips.
"Don't listen to him," he says.

Khaled squeezes my hand
and stares down at the sand.

I know,

despite his words,

he's just as hurt as me.

GATHERING

When I told Aisha the next day,
her hands made fists.
She was mad for me
and for her.
"Come on, Samira, tell them,"
Aisha says, nudging my arm.
Maya, Rubi, and Nadia fix their eyes on me,
waiting to hear the cause
of my beach outburst.
News travels quickly in Cox's Bazar.

The boy's voice rings in my ears
as we sit on a grass bank by the lake.
I tell them what happened,
but I can't stop.
Like a running tap,
it keeps coming.
I tell them how I lost everything:
my home
my land
my grandparents.

Rubi leans over and hugs me gently.
"At least you shouted back, Samira.
You showed how brave you are."

"There is nothing worse than losing
your family and home,"
Aisha says, staring at the lake,
her eyes filling with tears.
I think she's on the verge of
saying more, sharing what she's told me,
but she doesn't.

Nadia tucks in strands of her hair
loosened by the wind.
"I am sorry you've both lost family.
I can't imagine how terrible it must feel."
She pauses a moment.
"You know, things have not been
easy for us, either.
Ever since our baba lost his job
selling clothes at the market,
he puts more pressure on Tariq
to help support our family.
And that makes my brother so moody."
Nadia looks at me sideways,
and just as I think she's finished,
she continues.

"His rentals don't bring in much money,
so he's got to look for work now."

I know how worry
can wear you down.
Part of me thinks
that's why Tariq is unkind
and controlling,
like with the surfboards.
But Maya reads the other
part of my mind.

"Still, he shouldn't be so mean," she says,
her arms crossed.
"He's just like my brothers.
Before they got married and left home,
they were always bossing me around."

Rubi plucks at a blade of grass.
"You're lucky to have siblings,"
she says.
"I'd do anything to have a brother or sister.
Of course, I'd have to look after them.
Mama sews for ten hours,
then she delivers to the market.
I've even seen her fall asleep
without eating all day."

When each girl
tells their story,
it makes me think
we walk the beach together,
we sell our wares together,
but we share a lot more.
I'm beginning to see
what else we all have
that's the same.

NIGHTTIME

Voices fill our house
as neighbors gather.
They ask about the news report
and what's happening at home.
Not everyone has access
to a radio or TV.
Our words feel heavy
and come slowly,
but sometimes
sharing
can soothe an aching heart.

Baba and Khaled step outside to mend
the neighborhood's blocked latrine,
while we discover more about home inside.
Mothers in touch with loved ones
back in Burma
tell us in hushed voices what they know.

"They come by night," they whisper.
"Though the Bangladesh government says
refugees have stopped coming,

the boats continue to arrive when it's dark
to avoid being arrested by Bengali coast guards
or shot by Burmese border troops."

With these pieces of information,
we each form a picture
of what's happening,
where's safe,
who's alive,
but never
why there's no change
for the better.

ALL AT ONCE

Tonight, I wrap myself
extra tight in my blanket.
As Nani would say,
it feels like
even tigers shiver
in winter.
But I wonder if it's my mixed-up mind
that is giving me the chills.

Unlike so many,
I have a mother
a brother
a father.
And we are alive and well
and together.
That does not erase what we've
endured,
lost.
I am grateful and angry
all at once.

FETCHING WATER

Me and Aisha carry containers
to fetch water from the well.
Aisha likes to lead the way.
"Follow me," she says,
veering off the path
and past a row of houses
I've never walked by before.

Looking up, I see kites
made of plastic and bamboo,
attached by string to children.
Kids my age walk barefoot along the path,
babies clinging to their waists.
A group takes turns sledding
down a dirt hill
on empty vegetable oil containers
split open.
If, no, WHEN, Sahara comes,
we'll try it.
And Aisha.

"There's a shortcut here. Come on."
Aisha speeds up,
and I'm panting just following her,
turning down alleyways,
making a left, then a right,
then another left.
She swerves past a pile of trash
and leaps over an open drain,
moving like a big cat.

She clearly knows this maze well.
"Wait, slow down.
I can't keep up."
Aisha stops, and I almost crash into her.
"This reminds me so much of the city," she says.
"When Baba and Dada were working,
I'd explore.
I knew where to go,
when to find the best food."

"In Yangon?" I ask, breathing hard.
"Yes," Aisha replies.
"I'd watch as traders set up their stalls,
filling their barrels
with vegetables or fruit.
And I'd wait for the right moment
to ask for spare food."

Aisha's eyes glow.
"They'd give me mangoes
so ripe they were almost rotten,
but still sweet and delicious.
I'd never refuse them."

In half the time it normally takes me,
we arrive at the well—a faucet
sticking out of a concrete slab in the dirt.
We fill our containers just in time.
Soon, a line forms behind us.

"Tell me more, Aisha.
I've never been to the city.
What else did you do?"

Our walk back is slower.
Every so often, we stop
to adjust our grip
or shake a numb hand,
and Aisha tells me
about cafés serving Italian coffee,
boutiques with fancy clothes,
luxury shops with shiny Swiss watches,
and taxis zooming along the streets.

Our lives have been so different,
mine and Aisha's.
She's a city girl
I'm a farm girl
and now our paths meet.

It took abandoning our homes
fleeing Burma
losing family
surviving the journey
to find each other
in this place by the sea.

A DARE

Mama wipes beads of sweat
from my cheeks with her palms.
"Maybe no selling eggs today," she says.
I brush her hand from my face,
"I'll be fine, Mama.
Don't worry."
Even fetching water early
in the morning
is hot work,
and now the long walk
to the beach will feel longer.
But it's worth it
to have cool sea air
on my skin.

Aisha waits for me in the woods.
"Come on, let's jump in."
I grab her hand, and we rush into the sea together.
"Not too far out," says Aisha.
She's not a strong swimmer
and never stays long in the water.

Back on the beach,
Aisha lies on the sand,
her arms spread out.
I stay floating in the sea
and watch the surfers.
Rubi and Nadia
wait for waves.
Maya leaves their side
when she sees me.
She comes in closer,
and calls out,
"Want to try?"

My heart races,
and a spark inside me
ignites.

It's just like my first bike ride.
Sahara found an old bike,
and we flipped a coin
to see who went first.
I called flower,
Sahara agreed to monkey,
and when the coin landed
on flower, I grew nervous.
Only two wheels of rubber
touching the ground!

How can you stay on?
I gripped the handles,
pushed my foot down, and took off.
My tires made a wobbly snake trail
in the dirt.
Sahara tried,
knees coming up high
because her legs are longer,
and we giggled all afternoon,
taking turns.

"I'll ask Nadia if you can try mine."
I shake my head at Maya's offer
and leave it at that.
I wonder how long I can
hush the voice inside me
that cries out
yes.

WHITE PAPER

I wait patiently
to dive into my salty dahl.
Mama and Baba insist we wait for Khaled.
My stomach doesn't understand
this rule.

Outside comes a shuffling noise.
Our door swings open,
and my tastebuds and tummy
are finally happy.
"Look what I have!"
I think he's talking about
the rice he brings from the café
wrapped in silver foil,
but Khaled unrolls some white paper.
I scoot over to make space for him on the mat.
"This is just a rough copy,"
he says, "but it's a flyer
for a surf contest.
Mr. Ali let me have it.
He's helping put it together."
And Khaled points to some numbers

on the top line.

“There’s prize money! Tk.10,000!” he says.

“Samira, eat.”

Mama’s words pull my eyes

from their feast.

“It’s the best ever tonight, Mama.

And just the right amount of salt.”

I quickly lower my gaze,

scoop up my dahl.

Eyes can show a lot, Nana once said.

They are the wells of our lives,

carrying our stories,

hiding our secrets,

cradling our dreams.

Make sure you trust your onlooker, he said.

Only now do I know what he meant.

The flyer, the contest, the invitation, the prize money.

I am dizzy,

and I can't let anyone see.

INVITATION

Why not?
I could learn to surf
before the contest in six months.
My mind races with the daring
and dreaming
of what could be.

Khaled writes
about the contest,
I'm guessing,
about what he'd buy with the winnings.
A cricket bat, his own surfboard,
a new notebook, a bigger pot for Mama,
enough betel leaf to last Baba a lifetime.
A new house?

I clear my throat.
"I read the word 'girls' on the flyer."
"That's right," says Khaled.
"Girls are invited to enter the contest, too."
"Do they mean any girl?" I ask.

Our eyes lock.

"Samira, you can't surf."

I turn on my side,

my back an armor to his words.

The wall feels kinder.

It becomes my canvas, and in broad strokes,

the letters say *G-I-R-L-S.*

But all I see is *S-A-M-I-R-A.*

IN BETWEEN MOMENTS

Wet blankets sway on a breezy day.
My hands are doing the hanging,
alongside Mama's.
My body is here,
but my mind is far away.
It strings together letters in midair,
forming *the, these, those.*
Important, rule-breaking words
because *t* says *tuh* and *h* says *huh,*
but together, tongue on teeth,
they make a silly, tickly sound.

Mama smiles at the pile of drying laundry.
What would she think if she knew?
Washing clothes helps our family,
selling eggs helps our family.
Reading will help us, too.

BROKEN RULES

Racing to madrasah.
Playing where Burmese soldiers linger.
And now add reading and swimming.
I've always stepped on rules
gently,
like tiptoeing around puddles
to avoid getting wet.

School and work
before
getting married,
that's the path I want to walk.
A path built from
your very own dreams, Nana had said.

Now, that path is windy
and strewn with hurdles.
Mama and Baba would wonder
why I have dreams different than theirs
why I want to read and swim.

I would tell them
breaking rules doesn't always lead to
bad things.
I would show them
breaking rules can lead to
wonderful things.

SWEEP

As Baba fixes our ripped roof
and Mama rinses dishes,
I sweep the floor.
With each stroke,
I make my case.

"Baba, learning is good, isn't it?"
"Very good. Yes," he agrees.
Swish-swish.
"Like learning to cook for the family," I say.
"Yes, of course," he says.
Swish-swish.
Mama brings in her clean silver pot.
"And you'll be a good cook when you're older."
"No!" Baba interrupts, eyes smiling.
"She's already a good cook!"

Baba's stern *no* scares me at first,
and then
his praise makes me relax.
Maybe telling them won't be
so bad.

OPEN PALM

Courage is like a feather in an open palm:
gone with the smallest puff.
What if they say no?
What if they make me stop?
What if reading and the water,
like Nani and Nana,
are taken from me?
I close my hand
until my courage
can brave any storm.

PLAYTIME

Aisha crouches and takes slow, wide steps
toward a tamarisk tree.
Once there, she surveys the area.
"Well, can you see them?"
Nadia calls out.

Aisha shrugs.
"Make double sure.
How about the far end?
I've seen police there."
Nadia points down the coast.

"They might be having lunch
or taking a break," Maya suggests
as she chews on bread.
Rubi wipes shells
with the end of her orna
and pretends to admire her
reflection in the sheen.
"It's too early for lunch."
Maya pouts at her.
"How do you know?"

"Shhh!" Nadia sneers at them.
"Stop arguing."
The talk of food
must have set her off.
Nadia holds her growling belly
as she eyes the eggs in my bucket.
"Take one," I say,
"it's yours."
Nadia reaches for it
and then stops.
"But then you'll
have one less to sell,
and . . ."
I drop it in her hand,
and Nadia smiles.
It's the biggest smile she's ever given
to me, at least.
Rubi insists she's not hungry
when I offer her a snack,
and Maya says she's full of bread.

Nadia shakes her head no
when Maya points to her bucket;
my egg is enough to fill her up.
I might lose money by sharing
an egg or two,
but right now,

making friends
feels more important.

Aisha casually steps out from hiding
and onto the beach.
She stretches and yawns.

"All clear," says Nadia.
"Let's go. Rubi, don't forget your shells."
Rubi grabs her bucket,
and as she dashes out from the tree,
her foot catches on some roots.
She trips, sending her shells
into the air.

"You're the clumsiest person, Rubi!"
says Maya as she helps her up.
We burst into giggles,
even Rubi.
"I wanted to jump in first," she explains.
"Too bad, because I'll be the first."
I take off running,
diving into the water,
followed by Nadia,
whose cheeks bulge with egg.
After Rubi picks up the shells

and carries Maya's bucket for her,
they join us.

"There you are."
A boy's voice calls out behind us.
Khaled races from the woods
and into the sea,
sending a spray of water to my face.
This is one of those times
when my brother
is annoying
and embarrassing.
I have no choice
but to get him back.

VICTORY FEELS LIKE

Victory feels like
my mouth wrapping itself
around new sounds and words.
Victory feels like
meeting new people, making new friends.
Victory feels like
my skin cooled from the water,
wet hair, tired limbs.
Victory feels like
me.

CAUGHT

Baba's voice booms.
"What is this, Samira?"
His black locks shake,
his eyes glare.
"Your hair is wet!"

My excitement
made me forget
what it means for an older girl
to be in the water.
My bliss
made me forget
to dry my hair,
get rid of the evidence.
Both are snuffed out
like a candle flame.
"Baba, I . . ."

"Tell me you weren't in the water."
Mama's voice trembles with anger.

"Do you know how dangerous it is,

how you can drown?"

Mama knows

I know.

I was on the boat, too.

"Samira was helping me," Khaled says.

I could have been.

But Mama and Baba know the truth.

"I needed help with my surfboard."

It is possible.

Mama and Baba know.

"And she got splashed with water."

Highly likely.

Mama and Baba know.

I break out in a sweat

as Mama tells me and Khaled

to be quiet

and sit down.

I find a spot on the mat

and think about how swimming,

and maybe even reading,

will be gone forever.

I glance at Khaled

and wonder if

what's about to come

will make it into his notebook.

LOVE SONG

If only Nani and Nana were here.
When we left our village,
Mama said, *Only take the bag you packed.*
We have to go this minute.
Mama and Baba had two bags
next to the front door,
ready for this moment.

But I never believed it would come.
My bag was not ready.
I was not ready
to run away from our home,
from a place we'd always believed
to be safe.

Nani waited while I ran back
for my blanket.
She understood.
She knew it meant
comfort to me.

Nana pointed to his small bundle.
He'd carry my treasure
until I needed it.

Later, Nani talked to Mama, using words
tender like a love song,
and Mama listened without anger.

Sometimes, I miss Nani's love song
so much
I could crack.
If only Nani and Nana were here.

PASSED DOWN

Mama and Baba say I am just like
my grandparents.

My hair is fine and long
like Nani's.
My eyes are big and round
like Nana's.

That's not
what they mean,
though.

They're talking about my nature,
stubborn
and curious.

Fetching and hiding the blanket.
Me, Nani, and Nana,
we all broke the rules.

Mama and Baba are right.
I am just like my grandparents.

BLESSED

Baba clears his throat.
"Khaled, Samira, you both know
how difficult things are."
As if giving a lesson,
Baba speaks slowly.
"To be here in Bangladesh
alive
is to be blessed."

Mama takes out a torn map.
She points to the Naf River,
her finger pushing north to show
how far we traveled.
"After crossing," she says,
"we kept going until we found work
to make a better life
for you and Khaled."

When Mama and Baba talk
about our home in Burma,
a faraway look settles in their eyes.
Eyes say everything, just like Nana told me.

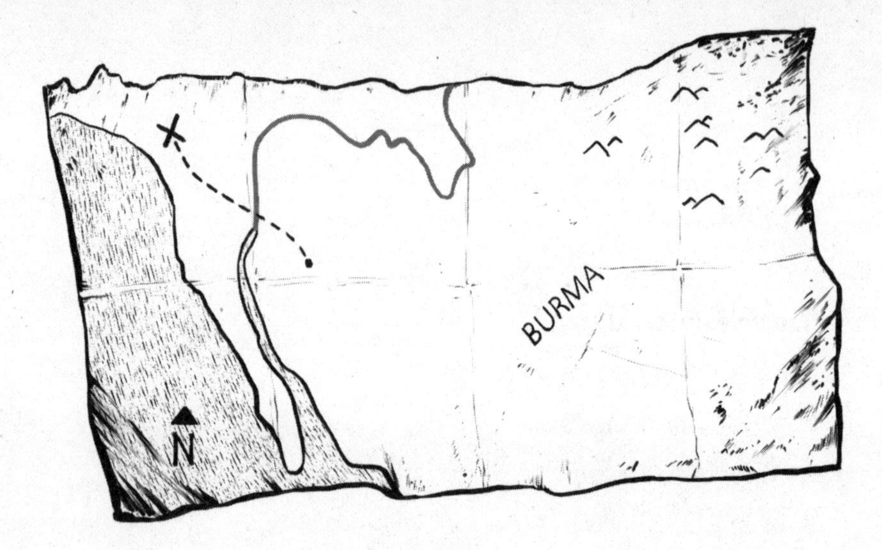

"Those who stayed are in danger.
And those who left took a chance
with their lives."
Mama pauses and stares at me,
then Khaled.

We are listening
with more than our ears.
Our hearts can hear, too.

"We survived," Mama continues,
"We are safe, and we can't throw away
this second chance."
She is right.
"No risk means no danger.
A girl swimming will start gossip,
and gossip will cause trouble.

The police could report us
and throw us out of Cox's Bazar,
out of Bangladesh,
and where will we go?"

But does that mean
we have to keep watch
all the time,
knowing our existence
will offend others no matter what?
I only whisper this question
inside.

Mama's voice hardens.
"No swimming for you, Samira."

Baba lets out a deep breath
and gives me a kind look.
Next, he turns to Khaled and says,
"And you, don't encourage your sister.
It will only bring her pain."

Khaled glances my way.
I want to tell him
it's not his fault,
it didn't happen because of him,
it's me who wants more.

COST

Mama and Baba's words
play over and over in my mind
as I lie snug in Nani's blanket,
running my fingers along the stitches,
following them as far as I can.

From what I can see,
being safe and alive
means having no freedom.
Is this the only way to live?
Can someone tell me?

If Nani were here, she'd talk to Mama and Baba.
Go easy on them, they're still young, she'd say.
Don't squash their hope.
The corners of Nani's eyes would crinkle,
and Mama would let out a deep breath.

Nana would bring wisdom.
One time he asked,
What gives a person the power
to walk through a wall?

When I couldn't find the answer,
he replied, *A door, of course.*
Nana would show us that door,
and if there were
no door,
he'd make one.

I thought my grandparents would always be here
to show us the way.

SHARP EDGE

"Come quickly!" Aisha calls out.
"It's your Baba. He's hurt."
One minute, me and Mama prepare dinner,
the next minute,
we run.
Water sloshes out of the bowl,
rice spills on the floor,
dust kicks up.

Aisha arrives first.
She points to a coconut palm
where the boys usually play cricket.
Baba slumps against its trunk in the shade.
Sweat runs down his face,
pools in his neck creases.
His chest rises
and falls
in shallow breaths.

"My back," he tells us.
"I have a shooting pain,
and it feels like it's on fire."

Me, Mama, and Aisha put our arms around him
and heave up a mass
of tired bones and slack muscle,
a frame somehow smaller than I remember.

On our journey uphill,
Baba flinches, so we slow down.
The tears I blink back
come from a different kind of pain.
A pain that makes me feel
like life will forever teeter
on a sharp, sharp edge.

STILL

In Burma, Baba came home
with stories of his day in the paddies.
Feeling earth between his fingers,
whispering to the seeds he planted,
watching sprouts stretch toward the sun
made him proud.

Here, he works on a shrimp boat,
six or seven days a week,
laboring twice as hard as the Bengalis.
An empty net means no pay.
"We'll manage," Baba always says.
Yet the Bengalis get paid regardless.
"It's not fair," Mama insists.

But we have no choice.
They call us refugees,
and refugees can't work
legally.

Low pay, long hours.

"Any job is better than no job," Baba reminds us.

But *still*, Mama's eyes say.

Still.

ONLY CHANCE

Baba looks
like he is sinking
into an older body.
I know he is young,
but I don't remember his age.
Is he 30?
I have no way to check.
Our ID cards
sank to the bottom of the river.
Never mind, Mama had said,
they weren't the good ones.
The papers showing our age
and Burma as our birthplace
are long gone.
The government took those.

Before his eyes close,
Baba tells us how he slipped,
how he struck his back
on the side of the boat.
Boats are not stable,

like the earth in the rice paddy
back home.

My brother arrives home early.
"How is he?" he whispers.
Mama frowns.
"He's hurt and in pain.
How will he get better?
How will we survive?
You'll have to work more, Khaled.
There's no other way.
You're our only chance."

"Of course." Khaled nods.
He straightens his back and gives Mama
a serious look,
like he can take the extra pressure.

How about me?
How about my work?
And Mama,
there is another way.
If I learn to surf and
win the surf contest,
the prize money could change our fate.
I could also be our chance.

Khaled lies down on his sleeping mat,
his back turned to me,
notebook in hand.
He sobs quietly and writes,
slow at first, then faster.
Only his notebook knows
what he carries inside.

I plug my ears with my fingers
because I know any minute
I'll cry, too.

OUR HISTORY

Khaled helps Baba
get up from the floor,
walk around,
use the latrine.
He comes home late from the café,
the smell of spices in his hair.
And he stays up
even longer,
writing,
drawing.

Is this his way to be close to Nana?
When I ask him,
he tells me he wants
to record things
so he can share them when he's ready,
so others will know what we have endured,
so our history is never forgotten
because our stories are told
and not written.

Then he admits, it's also his way,
of spending time with Nana,
whose life continues
with each word and picture.

A VEIL

Baba will get better,
and I will sell mountains of eggs
and we will have an ocean of salt.
My bucket, heavier these days,
means more eggs
more hope
for money.

But Mama is beyond my reach.
A veil of silence falls over her,
like the one I saw before we left Burma.

ESCAPE

I covered my ears from the *pa-pa-pa*
and the screaming.
Who did they shoot?
I'm too scared to open my eyes.
Soldiers torched homes
our mosque
our market.
Smoke curled around our throats,
squeezing.

So we fled with neighbors
into the blackness of night,
terror biting down hard.
I glanced behind
to see if it was all true.
"Samira, keep your eyes ahead," Baba called out.

We walked through forests
I knew as well as
the lines in my palm,
going at Nani and Nana's pace,

slowly,
resting often,
restarting only when they were ready.
Every time we heard
the rumble of cars,
or trucks,
we hid and waited until
the path ahead was clear.
A journey that normally takes
hours took days.
But we kept going
until water stretched before us,
unlimited.

We found the man
who took people across the river.
He'd been busy for weeks,
he said,
going back and forth
as more people fled
by day or night.

We paid him, and the murky river
carried us away
to Bangladesh,
Mama clinging to my arm,

Nani and Nana side by side,
Baba and Khaled sitting behind,
dirt on their faces.

We didn't know
what lay ahead,
we only knew
what lay behind
was no longer bearable.

ELSEWHERE

I am at the beach,
but my heart is at home
loving Baba.
My hands are at home
helping Mama.

Maya pulls me back.
Aisha, Rubi, and Nadia are with her.
"So many people today!"
Maya looks at the crowd gathering
before the midday heat.

On any other day, I would be glad
to hear the chatter
and splashing.
It means I could sell lots of eggs.
Instead, I lower my head
and try my best
to blink back tears.

"Samira! Samira!"
I can't help it.

I sink into the sand.
"Are you tired?"
Maya searches my face for answers.
"It's my baba," I say.

Their expressions tell me
they have heard from Aisha.
So I don't waste time explaining.
"I've never seen him so frail.
What if he doesn't get better?
What if, just like Nani and Nana . . ."
I can't help but sob.

"Don't think like that," Nadia says,
wiping my cheeks
and rearranging my orna.

"I'll pray that he gets better quickly
and you'll get through this
and you'll sell plenty of eggs."
Rubi gently lays her hand on mine.

Aisha grabs my bucket
and moves it to the shade.
"Take some chips," she says,
"Just something extra to eat."

She grabs two handfuls
and drops them into my bucket.
"Here, have some bread, too,"
Maya offers.
"It will give your baba energy."

And just when I begin
to feel hope,
Nadia says, with a serious face,
"My mama and baba struggle as well.
None of you offered to help us.
Why?"

There are a few moments of silence
between us.
I'm all mixed up inside,
and all I know is that
my friends are reaching out,
and holding their hands
makes me feel better.
Nadia's hands are in her pockets,
cold and clenched.

It's Rubi who answers Nadia's
question.
"The one thing we've not had to go through,"

she says, "is losing our home.
Or being chased out of our
country."

Maya's eyes wander to Aisha
and me.
Then she slowly nods.

Nadia stands up
and looks down the beach.
"Come on, let's get to work."
One by one we join her,
and I offer a small smile.
But Nadia doesn't notice
or choses to ignore it.
I'm not sure which.

PROMISE

A ghostly Baba refuses to eat,
lies on his mat,
skinny.
Instead, he replays
how he slipped.

A man named Abdul
who works on the boat
said his wife and two children
set off across the river from Burma,
clinging to big plastic containers.
He had come first, to work
and send back money
for their journey.
His family followed two weeks later,
when it became too dangerous to stay.
The two-and-half-mile crossing
was long.

Not one of them made it.

Baba lost his footing

during that part of the story.

Even now as he tells us,

his blank eyes drift over to our silent meal.

They meet Mama's—hers rarely leave his.

Without money for medicine,

Baba has to bear the pain.

I must sell two buckets of eggs tomorrow.

I make a promise

to myself.

WONDERING

"I hope they're safe."
Mama's soapy hands
scrub the inside of the silver pot.
Strands of loose hair fall over her face.
She pushes them behind her ear
with the back of her hand.
Khaled looks at me.
I don't know who she's talking about either.

"Yes, of course, they must be."
Mama mutters again.
Then she comes out of her bubble
and sees us staring.

For the first time in so long,
Mama talks about home.
About her sisters and brothers
and our family
who dreamed of a Burma
where all Buddhist teachers
are kind to our children,
where police at checkpoints

let us leave our village
to see the doctor . . .
if you trusted your life
in their hands.
"I wonder," she says,
"did enough people around the world
see the news reports?
Do they know
we're being attacked?"

And I'm curious, too,
if anyone knows,
if anyone truly understands.
I glance at Khaled,
and he doesn't look sad.
Instead, a grin spreads across his face,
as though he's just had an idea.

ALL OF ME

I thought life would be easier here.

But it's not.

I wonder if it's hard because

I'm me

I'm a girl

I'm a Rohingya girl

I'm a Rohingya girl living in Bangladesh.

All these things are me.

They are woven together

and to divide them

is to no longer be

Samira.

PRAYERS

With his palms open in prayer,
eyes squeezed shut and lips whispering,
Khaled prays longer tonight.
After washing and covering my head
with my orna, I say my own prayers.
Relieve Baba of pain.
Bring back smiles and laughter.
Let them flow
so Mama can bathe in them, too.
And please, please,
may Khaled be rewarded
for his hard work.
If I pray hard enough,
these things will come.
They have to.

MEMORY

Khaled has no time to teach
reading and writing,
so I must teach myself.
"Keep swimming," he says,
"So your muscles don't lose their memory."

I set down my extra-heavy bucket
and scratch the dirt with a stick.
But no words come to me,
only Mama and Baba's stern faces.
If they knew what Khaled is teaching me,
they'd be angry
they'd try to stop us.

Maybe they'd insist no more friends.
And then what?
What would I do?
How would I spend my day?

Always tell the truth,
I learned at the madrasah.
Now, I'm scared to tell the truth,

and to lie,
so I do the only thing
possible in this moment.
I toss my stick away
and wait for the girls.

THREE FEET

Mama makes the dahl watery
so Baba,
now sitting up,
can drink it.
It's a brilliant idea.
We pour our dahl into Baba's
because he needs it more.

"Delicious!"
Baba's voice startles us.
We all rush over,
eager to hug and smother him
with love and tears of relief.

Mama's hand bars us.
No, we must not crowd him.
She approaches,
squats down,
buries her face in Baba's chest,
like she's checking his heartbeat.

And we love him

three feet away

with our gasps and smiles.

TOMORROW

Khaled comes home late,
a drizzle
bringing out the smell
of chicken curry and rice
on his damp clothes,
and its spicy aroma reminds me
of saalan.

"Did you bring any leftovers, Khaled?
You're making me hungry!"
I roll over and see his empty hands.

"Shh!" Khaled crouches by me.
"I have to talk to you," he whispers,
reaching behind his back
to pull out something
tucked into the waistband
of his pants.

"You have a cell phone!
Where did you get that?"
A proud smile spreads across his face.

"Mr. Ali loaned it to me
until tomorrow.
We can call home!"

I am so excited,
I push my blanket to one side
and jump up.
"But we have to wait," says Khaled.
"Mama and Baba are sleeping.
Let's call in the morning."

This is how my brother can be
sensible and smart—
and annoying!
Tomorrow cannot come
quickly enough.

Before the song of cha,
Khaled gets up
and stands by his sleeping mat,
eyes shut, palms cupped.
It's the shortest prayer,
but I'll tell no one!

When Khaled grabs the phone,
he lets out a groan

so loud, I think he's hurt.
"The battery is low.
I didn't think about
turning it off last night.
I can't believe I forgot."
Lips pressed together,
Khaled shakes his head.

"Don't worry," I say quickly.
"Let's tell Mama and Baba.
We'll make the call
as soon as they come back."

Mama is out walking
with Baba.
Rebuilding his muscles
is important, she says.
Baba agrees, and together
they stroll along the path,
and Baba always returns,
cheeks flushed and smiling.

The door swings open,
and we spring to our feet.
"We have something for you."
Khaled holds out the surprise.

I've never heard Baba's voice go squeaky.
"A cell phone! I can't believe it.
Where did you get it?"
He smiles, showing red-stained teeth.
I missed them!
Mama, hand on her chest,
draws in a sharp breath.

Khaled tells them about Mr. Ali
and insists we call
right away.

"I know it's here somewhere."
Mama mumbles as she looks in a bag.
"My notepad has all the phone numbers."
She tips the bag out on the floor
and rifles through its contents.
"Here, I'll help," Baba offers,
but when his back says no,
he stays seated.

Me and Khaled sift through
pieces of our old life strewn on the floor.
Family photos,
receipts from selling our crops,
an old Quran bound in dark green leather
with a gold border

passed down in our family,
a bundle of hijabs,
Mama's jewelry from her wedding,
and silver nose rings from Nani.

The thought of hearing
Auntie's voice again
and learning how everyone is doing
makes hope crawl up my spine,
makes me feel strong.

NUMBERS TO NOTHING

Mama flips the other bag upside down.
She pushes aside Baba's clothes.
"Got it," she says,
picking up a black notepad
small enough to fit in her palm.
Its cover is tattered,
its pages yellow,
and the numbers faint,
black ink eaten up by moisture.
"Thank God," she whispers.
"Hasina's number is still here."
Khaled picks up the phone.
We are ready.
But my brother's face
turns pale,
his jaw drops,
and he announces,
"The battery is dead."

LIFELINE

Baba surprises us sometimes.
Without warning,
he throws a net below our feet
when we are falling
from a mountaintop.

Without a phone charger,
we can't make the call.
"It doesn't matter," he says.
"We can call tomorrow.
Ask Mr. Ali if he can charge it for us."
Mama remains quiet.

"But, Baba, I wanted . . ." Khaled starts.
"One day makes no difference,"
Baba interrupts.
"Besides, we need to think
about what to ask,
you know,
small details."
And Mama forces a smile. "Yes, it'll give us time."

Think about our questions?

Mine are on the tip of my tongue.

Are you safe? Are you all together?

What about our house?

How are the chilis and rice in the paddies?

Are the markets open again? What about schools?

And my list,

it has

no end.

DANGLING

Khaled comes home from the café
at the end of the longest day.
Me and Mama and Baba
wait on the mat.
"Are you ready?" he asks.
I was ready yesterday.

Khaled gives Baba the phone.
Slowly, Baba taps the numbers,
then holds the phone to his ear.
We lean in.
"It's ringing," he reports.
"Don't forget to ask about Sahara,"
I remind him.

Baba's lips move,
but I can't hear his words,
my heartbeat is so loud.
I try to read his eyes,
to see what they can tell me,
just like Nana said.

Baba closes the phone
abruptly.
That's it?
Just a few minutes?
What about all the questions
I wanted to ask?

The line was bad,
it was hard to hear,
Baba tells us.
Everyone is fine,
but more soldiers patrol the villages,
spreading fear and panic.
No one knows who to trust,
which story to believe.
Our family has been rounded up
and forced into a camp
not far from the village.

"They're in a camp?
Can't they come here?" Mama asks.
"They say it's impossible
to leave," Baba replies.
"Soldiers guard the camp,
so for now, they must stay."

Then Mama asks a question
that gives me goosebumps.
"Did they ask about Nani and Nana?"
Baba says nothing,
but his gaze wanders to Mama,
and she rocks back and forth,
back and forth,
her chin trembling.

Baba's eyes meet mine.
"No one has seen Sahara and her family."
These words
feel like a slap.

What does that mean?
Are they hiding?
Were they moved to a camp as well?

But I choose to cling
to what Khaled says next.
"Maybe they're coming to Bangladesh,
maybe they all will,
and soon we'll be together
like we used to be."

I AM NOT

"There, their, they're."

Khaled makes the same sound

three times.

"Yes, I heard you!"

"Samira, what's wrong with you today?"

It could be the weather

that's making me irritable.

The humidity feels like

a wet cloth against my skin.

But I know it's not that.

My whole family and best friend

are trapped.

I cannot

sit and talk with them

share a meal with them

be in the same country as them.

All the things I'm not allowed

stack up.

Under their weight,
I am collapsing.
On the surface we are
a brother and a sister trying to
live our lives.
But underneath, we are
jumbled thoughts
and longing.

Khaled picks up his pencil
and scribbles angrily in his notebook,
pencil point racing over the page.

"Samira?" I hear Mama's voice.
Does she see us in our green cloak
and crown now turned gray with clouds?
I quickly stand up
behind the clump of tall grass
where we crouch.
To lose reading,
the one thing within my grasp,
would be unbearable.

Before I leave our spot,
what I see in Khaled's notebook

makes me shrink.
His heart lives
on these pages,
a heart I am still
getting to know.

MY BROTHER

Each day, Baba's back improves.
Since the phone call
he walks, bending down here,
twisting his back there,
without a grimace or wincing.
Soon he'll be back at work, he says,
but he looks at the sky and knows,
when monsoon season comes,
shrimping is even harder.
The boats become slick,
dampness sets into your bones,
and lightning makes the work
dangerous.

I continue to comb Baba's hair.
Even though he is better,
I still like to groom him.
"How is my Samira this morning?"
"I am good, Baba."
How can I tell him about my brother?
About the words and pictures from his notebook?

What Khaled keeps silent
roars on every page.
I WANT TO STAY.
THIS IS OUR HOME.
What he hides in shadow
becomes art on every page.
Guns aimed at babies,
mothers with faces twisted in horror.

My brother's worries may be different
than mine, but still, they torment him.

DIRTY WATER

Khaled was up last night.
He crept to the latrine,
and I know I shouldn't have done it,
but I did.

I listened.

On a still night, noise travels.
I heard a growl.
Is that distant thunder?
It comes again,
and I know it's Khaled.

Drink from the well, Baba tells us.
The water is cleaner.
But the line at the well has grown.
Even older women and young children
climb the steep hill to fetch water.
We are so thirsty,
we drink from the river
that feeds into the sea,
or a pond,

or even the lake where people
scrub their clothes and themselves.

When Khaled returns
after being sick,
I whisper, "Are you ok?"
"I'm fine," he snaps.
Sometimes I think Khaled hides the truth
because it's easier
than showing his pain.

SONG

When me and Khaled were younger,
Nana would sing us songs
and play the mandolin,
his fingernails, soiled from the paddies,
skipping across the strings.

With eyes squeezed shut,
he'd make up a song
and sing as if he'd known it
his whole life.

Sometimes, Nana would slow down
and open one eye
to make sure we were listening.

And when he saw each word and chord
soothing us,
he'd continue,
lips smiling
and fingers plucking.

If he were here,
I wonder which verse he'd sing,
because Nana always knew
the right balm
to heal our wounds.

WHY NOT?

Halfway down the beach,
a group of people surf.
I bet they're renting Tariq's boards.
Mr. Ali, close by, points to waves
and talks to people dressed like
they're from the city.
They stroll along,
scan the beach,
making notes on paper.
Who are they?
What do they write?

When I come closer,
I see Khaled.
"Here," he says,
handing me a silver foil package.
"I gave Tariq his portion,
and there was extra today."
Rasgulla!
Cheesy sweetness floods my mouth.
"Mmm. So delicious."
I wipe my sticky lips on my sleeve.

"What are those people doing, Khaled?"
He explains, "The Surf Bangladesh Committee
is meeting about the contest.
They're inspecting the area
so they can decide where to have it.
There's the tide and rip
to think about
and a lot to plan ahead of time."

And then Khaled's eyes get big.
"Did I tell you?
Mr. Ali's café will be making food
for the event."

One word sends my head spinning.
Contest.
The one where girls are invited?
The one with Tk.10,000 prize money?

I find a cozy spot
and watch my beach change from
the place where I work
to the place where I want to surf!

What if I am more
than an egg seller?
What if I am
Samira the Surfer?

TINY WHISPER

After dinner, Baba goes for a walk
by himself.
He no longer needs Mama's help.
His back is better,
and he has even returned to work.
Ever since Mama found her notepad,
she spends her evenings
looking through its pages.
I've learned that numbers can lead to
memories.

A candle burns close by,
bright enough for Khaled to write,
dim enough for me to fall asleep.
But I don't want to.
The surf contest is on my mind.

I've been brave before.
Like the time Sahara dared me
to open a coconut.
Baba told me to ask first
and he'd split one open

with his machete
so we wouldn't get hurt.
But I took the biggest one
I could find
and smashed it against
the sharp corner of a rock
over and over until
a spray of sweet coconut water
covered our faces,
and we collapsed in laughter.
Today, I felt the old me flicker,
the one who loved adventures.

I imagine myself
being so free
that I take to the water
to ride a wave.
And I know
what I feel
in this moment,
I cannot unfeel.

A NEW LANGUAGE

I put our morning reading aside.
"Tell me more about surfing,"
I ask my brother.
Khaled takes the magazine
from under his pillow
and turns to pages that show
pictures of a world unknown to me.
I see surfers on sea-glass blue waves,
beaches that look nothing like Cox's Bazar,
giant monster waves,
long boards, short boards.
And girls!
Lots of girls.
Every picture comes alive
as he explains.

Drop in,
bottom turn,
cut back.
I am learning a fourth language:
the language of surf!
Rolling in my mouth,

curling around my tongue.
When I spit them out,
I'm sounding, talking, feeling
more and more
like a surfer.

Names for parts of the board
bring smiles, too.
Nose, tail, leash like it's a puppy.
Rails like it's a train on tracks.
Deck like it's a boat.
Fin like it's a fish.

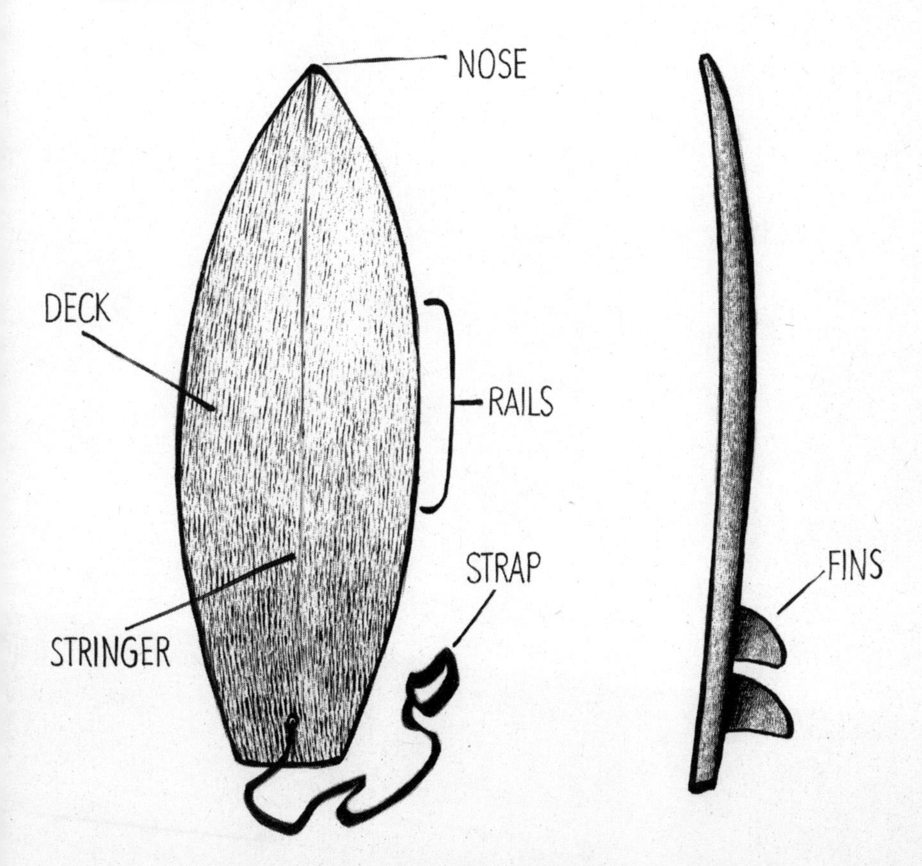

And everything Khaled shares with me
is sealed in my mind
to be remembered forever,
long after the magazine goes back
under his pillow.

MY VOICE

GIRLS INVITED
The letters, big and bright,
make impressions on my back
as I lay awake.
Baba told Khaled to put the flyer away.
Is it bad of me to hide it
under my sleeping mat?
I say no! What harm can it do?
It's just paper and hope.

To make sure I'm doing it right,
I look at Khaled's magazine,
then try myself.

I flip over.
With my head lifted,
I paddle until my arms feel sore
and my neck grows stiff.

Cluck, cluck, cluck.
Our chickens outside tease me.
I can't help but laugh

at them,

at myself.

A little voice in my head

that sounds like the younger,

stubborn Samira

pipes up loud and clear.

You can't give up, she insists.

Why not have fun

and play with the waves?

TREAT IN THE MARKET

Mama takes a black comb
and pulls its teeth though my hair,
making my scalp go tingly.
Next comes a gentle scrape across,
front to back,
with the end of the comb.
She makes a part,
her fingers work busily
at one side of my head,
then the other,
until I have two braids.

"Come to the market with me," she says.
"I need help bringing food home.
And see if Aisha wants to come."

We make a quick stop by Aisha's house.
Her dada is happy his granddaughter
has an invitation.
The corners of Mama's eyes smile
when she meets him.

Just like mine did
the time I first met him.

At the market we are pressed between
bright colors,
sharp smells,
and the hum of voices.

Mama hands a seller some coins.
Even in March, the air makes
flames against our skin.
Cool mango lassi
would be refreshing.
But soft roti would be filling.

My grumbling belly wants both.
Aisha decides on lassi, and I follow.
Tickets to heaven!

I hear foreign languages
spoken by aid workers
and news photographers
gathering at postcard and souvenir stands.
They buy seashells,
T-shirts, and maps of Cox's Bazar.
Will Khaled meet them
at the café? I wonder.

A snake of surfboards
weaves through the market.
I know this snake!
It's a group of boys balancing boards
on their heads.
Smiling surfer faces meet ours.

We step aside.
"So heavy." Mama makes a *tsk-tsk* sound.
"And the water's so dangerous.
Your Nani and Nana . . ."
Mama puts a finger to her lips
to stop the flow of words.

Aisha whispers in my ear.
"They remind me of Nadia, Rubi, and Maya."
I pretend not to hear,
for Mama is close by.
Aisha!
If Mama discovers my friends are surfers,
she'll know I want to be one, too.

My delicious lassi
turns sour.
My colorful market
fades to black and white.
I would trade them both

to take a risk on my terms

to be with my sisters

to be a kid

to feel free.

TUNE IN

Strong arms help you
carry the surfboard,
paddle,
get up on your feet.

But surfing is more than muscle power.
I learn from the beach,
studying Khaled, his friends, and the girls.
How they move in the water,
how they catch waves.
Every day, I see something new.

Water moves to its own
rhythm and beat,
but if I listen,
pay close attention,
I, too, can learn its music.

PICTURES

Aisha peers around the corner.
"Let's go to the beach," she whispers.
Baba says he's glad I have
a good friend
but tells me not to be long
when I ask to play with Aisha.

"If I had lots of money,
this is what I'd buy."
Aisha draws in the wet sand.
An airplane.
Of course,
to travel the world.
"What would you buy, Samira?"

I make my own dreams.
Books and pencils.
"That's it?"
I draw an oval.
Aisha squints.
I add a stick person,
and instantly she knows.

When Aisha sees my secret,

her jaw drops.

"Samira, you want a surfboard?

You want to surf?

You are so brave!"

Sharing my wish makes it feel

real.

ECHOING WAVES

"The waves aren't good today."
Nadia's voice is flat.
"I'm surprised they're out there."
She points to three boys
who chase small, choppy waves.

"They're probably desperate,"
Maya says, looking down at her sandy feet.
"I know how they feel."

We stand under a tree, but
its shade barely offers
relief from the blistering heat.

"When are you finally going to try it?"
Maya gives me a cheeky smile.
"You always watch."

"What's it like out there
in the middle of the sea?

What it's like standing on a board,
riding waves?"
I imagine it's a little scary,
but in a good way.

Maya squeezes her arms and legs.
"Surfing makes me feel
strong and powerful,
like I'm an athlete."
She grins. "It's hard to explain."
But I understand.

"With nothing but
calm, still water
around you," Nadia says,
closing her eyes.
"It's so amazing.
Then, a loud *shhh* noise
as the wave comes closer.
Out there, my mind is clear.
I don't think about anything."

When Nadia talks about the surf,
her voice goes soft, and she glows.
"You really look comfortable

out there," I tell her. "Like you were
meant to be riding waves."

Nadia smiles,
her cheeks blushing.
She likes my comment,
that I see her,
that I'm beginning
to understand her.

"When the waves are better,
maybe you can try surfing." Maya suggests,
glancing at me from the corner of her eyes.
"What do you think, Nadia?
Tariq will let Samira use a board.
I mean, why not?
He knows she's with us."

I look at Nadia
as she chews on her lip.
"I'm not sure my parents would let me."
I say this because it's true,
of course they wouldn't,
but also because it fills the silence.

Then Nadia replies,
"I could ask him."

These four words
plant a little seed of hope in me.
"Really? You would ask for me?"
Nadia smirks. "I'll try when he's in a good mood."

"I'd like that," I say casually.
Inside, I'm jumping up and down.
Then I ask her, "Do your parents mind you surfing?"
Nadia straightens her jewelry
even though it's already neatly arranged
in her bucket.

"Mine were angry when they found out."
Maya says, fiddling with the ends of her two braids.
"Ever since Mama chased me off the water,
I don't tell her or Baba when I go."
Maya shows us the seam along her shalwar.
"Look. You can barely see the stitching.
Lucky for us, Rubi sews our clothes when
they get ripped by the waves."

After searching for shells
in the shoreline,
Rubi joins us under the trees.
"My parents know I've tried it.
They just don't know how often I go," she says.
"Mama's busy sewing,

and Baba sells newspapers.
I don't know what I'd do without surfing."

Nadia finally lets out a sigh.
"Surfing makes everything better.
I really want to compete in the contest.
I just don't know . . ." Nadia's voice trails off.
A contest without her is hard to imagine.
She's the best surfer.

Fixing her eyes on Nadia, Maya says,
"We have to compete.
It's the first contest in Cox's Bazar,
and there's prize money."
Then she frowns.
"I just have to make sure my parents
don't find out."

It's comforting to know
I'm not the only girl
with precious secrets
tucked away
so no one can see
and say no!

By day's end, I arrive home,
my bucket still nearly full.

Mama plants a kiss on my cheek,
and Baba tells me not to worry.
But selling eggs is not on my mind.
Tonight, the echo of waves plays over
and over in my ears.

A GAMBLE

"Pick any one you'd like," Aisha says
as we trade eggs and chips
under the coconut palms.
It makes me think of Sahara
and our bangle swapping,
my green ones with white flecks
for her blue ones with silver lines.

I rip open a bag of red chilli–flavored chips
and eat mine Maya's way,
three in one go.
As I chew, yesterday's conversation
with the girls comes back to me.
I think about the risks Nadia,
Maya, and Rubi would be taking
just to surf in the contest.
Would they be sorry if they got in trouble?
Is it worth it?

I ask Aisha, "Have you ever done something
you've regretted?

Something you wish
you could take back?"

My friend gazes at the horizon,
as if it holds the answer,
and I'm not sure if
it's one of those times
when she's in another country
in her mind.

But then Aisha says,
"When Dada told our family
we had to leave Burma
because police were going door to door
rounding up Rohingya,
we packed our things and
left before things got worse."

Aisha pauses, as though she considers
stopping right there.
I hold my tongue, and she says,
"Just me, Mama, Baba, and Dada.
Dadi died years before.
Everyone else chose to stay."

Aisha continues,
"It took lots of bus journeys

and days of walking through paddies
and over hills.
And when we got to the border,
we had to wait for our turn to cross,
so we slept in a forest."
I lean in,
holding this moment
she's kept close to her
for so long.
"During the night,
soldiers came
and opened fire."

Aisha clears her throat,
and then after a moment's pause,
she tells me more.
"Me and Dada ran to see
if the border police had gone,
while Mama and Baba gathered our things.
That's when the gunshots got closer."

Tears flood Aisha's eyes,
and she looks at me.
"They should have come with us.
They should have left our things there.
We didn't need them.
Their lives were more important."

I put my arm around Aisha,
and she rests her head in the crook
of my neck and sobs.

Like me, Aisha knows how
some risks turn out.
I don't ask any more questions.
I am just here for my friend.

FIREWOOD

Baba arrives home early,
a pile of firewood
balanced over his shoulder.
Once a week, he chops down trees
with Rohingya men
and some Bengalis.
This is his second trip this week.
What is his plan for all this firewood?

A LIE

An eerie stillness hovers
over the marketplace today.
The threat of rain
keeps people at home.

A tooting close by startles me,
and I see a tom tom zoom away,
leaving behind a trail
of smoke and hate.
"You Rohingya dogs lie, cheat, and steal,"
shouts a passenger in the back.

Khaled turns this way and that.
The words, aimed at him,
are like sharp arrows.
"But I didn't steal anything!"
He throws his hands up in the air,
one of which clutches a bag of flour.
Paid for, I saw.
Marketgoers stop and whisper.

"Let's go."
Khaled ushers me along.
He reminds me of Mama's words.
Their constant ringing
already makes grooves in my mind.
Don't draw attention
to us.
Don't cause trouble
outside.

A swarm of angry bees buzz
in my belly.
We are not thieves!
We do not steal!

Like a river rushing over the edge
of a waterfall,
I want to spill the truth
for all to hear and see and know.
How we fear for our lives
how we cannot live freely
how we are judged
before we open our mouths.

We walk back in silence.
Before stepping inside,
we shake hands.

A promise to not tell Mama and Baba
and witness
their upset faces.
And as we shake, I feel choked up
with yet another secret to hold.

EVERY TIME

"That was quick!"
Mama's frown softens
as if she worries,
as if she frets
every time we are gone
without her or Baba.
How much can Mama take
before worry gobbles her up?

MOUNTING SECRETS

I'm beginning to feel
like a volcano,
secrets gathering like lava,
building and building.

I didn't plan to keep so much
hidden.
Reading, swimming, my surfing dreams.

And now,
a pact with Khaled
about the market.
And if I erupt,
what will that spewing do
to our lives?

READY

Head up, strong strokes,
keep going, don't stop.

I'm awake before my reading lesson
to practice surfing
on my sleeping mat.

Khaled stirs.
How long has he been awake?
He mocks me.
"Shhhh! Stop teasing!"
"You're ready," he declares.
I am?
Really?
Khaled says he will teach me,
and I smile, slowly.

Did I hear right?
My brother is offering
to help make my dream come true.
Did I hear right?

BALANCE

Khaled has said
how can I be scared
of something I haven't tried?
You can be scared
and still try,
I'm learning.

Khaled's board wobbles
from side to side
under my weight.
Its deck is covered in white wax.
"Try to find the center
so you're balanced."

That's exactly
what I am
doing!
I slip off the front of the board.
I slip off the back.

"You have to feel it!"

Feel
what, Khaled?

"The sweet spot."

I point to a red stripe
across the width of Khaled's board.
This is tricky. I need some help.
"Is it here?
Or is it . . ."

"No, no," he calls out.
"You have to *feel* how to balance it.
Surfing is all about feeling, Samira."

I'm like a balloon
with a leak.
I can do this,
pump it back up,
I can do this.

My shalwar kameez
is an anchor to the seabed.
Chop slurps the side of the board.
I flip over again.
Salty water floods my mouth.

From the beach,
it looks easy, simple, effortless.
From here in my head,
it's the most impossible thing.

FOUNDATION

Lesson one: How to find the sweet spot.
You need time
you need patience
you need more time.
It's just like learning to read.
A letter, two letters, a sound, a word!

That's how, a week later,
I find the perfect place on the board,
steady and sure.

I meet Khaled in the woods,
for a break in the shade.
Eggs and salt on my lips
never tasted so good!

PHANTOM

Before we leave,
I pick up Khaled's board,
run my fingers along its rails,
then stand it up.
Its tail crunches against
grains of sand.
With my arm around its back,
I feel like we are new friends.

Under my grip,
its surface is hard, solid, strong.
I feel a *zing-zing* charge of life.
"When can we go next?" I ask.
Khaled scratches his head.
"Well, tomorrow I want to surf.
If only you had your own board."

I tell Khaled, "Nadia asked Tariq, but he said no.
I guess I need to find something
he wants in exchange!"

A flash of excitement
crosses Khaled's face.
"Tariq told me he'd do anything
for a job at the café."
"Anything?"
"That's what he said.
I think I know how
I could get you a board."

A dog barks and interrupts
our conversation.
I send out my radar:
an expanse of sand
and nothing but trees.
No one's there.
Woof, woof.
The dog barks
at the phantom again.
He sees it, too!
I turn away,
set the board down,
and inch closer to my brother.

In the water,
I feel free.

Back on land,

I am followed.

I can't wait until the next

zing-zing.

GIFT

I crouch in our reading spot,
waiting for my teacher.
Khaled appears without his notebook.
"I don't have time right now,
but meet me in the woods in an hour!"
He takes off like a chased crab,
and the next sixty minutes last
a lifetime.

Once I arrive, I look through the trees.
"Here," says Khaled.
In his hands is a treasure.
"A surfboard for you to use."
Me?
"See this spot here?"
There's a rough gray bump on the rail.
"It had a ding on it,
but it's been repaired.
I know it's old and dusty,
but it works," Khaled adds.

I see no ding,
no dust.
In my hands is a jewel,
a yellow surfboard,
bigger than Khaled's,
perfect for me.

"Your plan with Tariq worked?"
My genius brother nods.

"Tariq told me his sister
asked if you could borrow one."
Khaled continues, "And he refused,
but when I talked about the café,
his eyes got big
and his face went serious."

"But now he won't need your rasgulla," I say.
"He'll have his own scraps.
You won't get to borrow a surfboard,
and me neither."

Khaled smiles, "Mr. Ali needs reliable help
for the contest.
Think of all the food surfers eat

and the extra people in town.
He trusts my recommendation,
and he'll only take Tariq on
after trying him out."

I think of Tariq's sweet tooth.
The café will be heaven to him.
"So I'll get to use a surfboard,
at least until the contest.
That's how much he wants a job there?"

Khaled nods. "I looked him in the eye,
and we shook hands."
I want to trust Tariq, too,
and believe his word is a promise.

I think Khaled has told me
all there is to say,
but he adds, "Tariq said, 'If your sister catches on to surfing
as quickly as you did to cricket,
Nadia will have competition,'
and he laughed."

Tariq worries about me
being a good surfer?
I wish!

My belly tingles

like I've guzzled lots of coconut water.

A surfboard

for me!

A BEGINNING

By counting to ten,
I steady my nerves
and relax my body.
As soon as I slip into the water,
a coolness washes over me,
and I feel
free.

I ease myself onto my board
and find a new sweet spot
because it's different than Khaled's.

But today there are no waves.
Khaled says I have to be patient
and wait.
Some days there's nothing to ride.
This is a surfer's life.

STICKY SQUARE

Slow like turtles,
me, Aisha, and Maya
trudge across the sand
to dip our feet in the sea.
Even though it's not yet midday,
we are hungry,
tired,
and thirsty.
Maya cups a handful of water
and pours it over her face.
I've never seen
her energy so low.

"Let's go down." Aisha points to the crowd
where Rubi sells her shells.
"What happened to Nadia today?" I ask.
"She's late. Should we wait?"

"Nadia's staying home," Maya announces
as we walk down the beach.
"She told her parents she'll never
get married, and it ended in a big fight."

"Nadia is almost fourteen,
and her parents will look
for her husband soon,"
Maya explains.

"If Nadia gets married,
it's one less mouth
for her parents to feed,
one less person to support."

Aisha frowns. "What about Tariq?"
"He doesn't earn much money
from board rentals," Maya says.
"He says he might have a job at a café now."

As Maya finishes her last words,
we catch up with Rubi
selling shells to a family.
I'm still thinking about Nadia,
but the family wants chips, bread,
and eggs.
We all got lucky!

I slip the change under some eggs
only to discover
something sticky and white
at the bottom of my bucket.

I hold it to my nostrils
and take in its fruity smell.
What's this wax doing here?
Khaled is so kind to me!
He left me another gift,
a secret between a sister and a brother.

I put the wax back
and wonder when I'll get to use it.
"You surf?" the woman asks.
I smile, and the girls gawk at me,

but I say nothing
until we walk away.

Maya's eyes go wide
when I explain how Khaled
arranged for me to use a board.
"Let's celebrate," she says.
"How about now?"
Aisha doesn't wait for an answer.
She grabs our wares
and sets them down.
Maya's fast legs take her
to the water first.
Rubi runs in next.
Splat! A belly flop.
"Well, are you coming?" she calls out.

Our parents will never know
because as we jump in,
a band of rainclouds
drifts over our heads.

I WONDER

Rubi sews Nadia's ripped sleeve.
"Your parents won't guess
you surfed," she brags.
Aisha asks as she admires Rubi's stitches,
"When will you go next?"

From our spot in the woods,
Nadia looks out to sea and the distant sky.
"Not today," she says gloomily.
"It feels like there could be lightning."

Maya squats up and down next to a tree.
She insists this helps her stand up
quicker on her surfboard.
"How's the reading going, Samira?"
She asks, out of breath from
exercising.
"Learned any new words?"
I fan myself with a leaf,
trying to shrug off the afternoon humidity.
"Yes, from Khaled's surf magazine."
Rubi looks up from her sewing.

"Teach us some.
We're surfers after all."

I teach them *leash*
and *cut back* and *rails*.
Maya and Rubi listen with all ears.
Even Aisha, who doesn't surf,
pays attention to each word.

But Nadia is restless.
She kicks up sand with her toes
and clears her throat
a few times.
I can tell something is bothering her.
"Is everything ok?"

Nadia turns to look at us,
but her lips stay sealed.

"You can tell us, Nadia."
Maya encourages her.
"You're like a big sister to us,
but big sisters need friends, too."

Nadia reminds me a little
of Khaled,
the way she keeps a lot

inside.

I wonder if showing her emotions

makes her think

she's weak.

Khaled has writing.

Nadia has surfing.

But I wonder

if she needs more,

if she needs something else.

And the real question is

does she trust us,

does she trust me

enough

to show the lining of her heart?

CLOSING THE CIRCLE

Nadia takes a big breath,
like what she's about to share
is tough for her.
"It's my parents," she admits at last.
"They are worried about me.
I must be a burden to them."
Nadia stares at her feet.

"You never told us that before," says Maya,
a hint of surprise in her voice.
Rubi's frown confirms
Nadia has never opened up to her either.
"Do you always feel like that?"

"Most of the time.
But when I'm on the water,
I don't even think about it,"
Nadia explains.

Aisha picks up a leaf
and fans herself.

"What makes you think
you're a burden?" she asks.

"I can tell, when Mama says
less time outside,
to help my reputation,
to help me get married.
But she knows we need
money from my jewelry sales.
It's an impossible situation."

Maya leans in. "What do you tell her?
What are you supposed to do?"
"Stop the questions!" Rubi
swats the air in front of Maya.
"Let's just listen."

"I don't know what to do."
Nadia's tone is
matter-of-fact,
but I know for her
to even say this much
is a lot.
"One thing is sure," she adds.
"If I have to stay indoors
all day,

I'll be so bored.
I can't stand the thought."

Maya motions for us
to gather around Nadia.
And as we close in
with our bodies,
we make a safe place
for her to be herself.

Nadia's sharing
has brought us together,
and for the first time
since I met the girls,
our friendship
feels complete.

A RIPPED SACK

A game of cricket is on,
and so is a girls' meeting.
Nadia was so clever to suggest this.
I think our talk yesterday helped.
We hang out and chat
and dodge cricket balls
and giant puddles.

Tariq is batsman.
When he looks straight at me,
I shrink,
and suddenly my mouth goes dry.
I am overcome with
despair because
I understand why he's worried,
frustration because
I still think he's a mean person,
joy because
he's letting me borrow a board,
mistrust because
it's in exchange for a job.

Aisha's voice rescues me.
She asks about the prize for the contest.
"Is it a lot of money?"
We explain how girls can enter
and win Tk.10,000!
And like grains of rice
spilling from a ripped sack,
my words just slip out.

"I'd love to enter the contest,
but I don't have that much time
to learn to surf
if I'm selling eggs."

Aisha jumps up. "I know."
She spins around, bursting with excitement.
"I can help you. *I'll* sell eggs while *you* learn."
In return, more eggs for Aisha and her dada.
"Now that Tariq's loaning you a board,
we can all go together," Nadia adds.
Maya and Rubi agree.

Our plan is hatched.
It's decided:

1. I will enter the contest.
2. Aisha will sell eggs for me.
3. Mama and Baba will never know.

A light drizzle begins
to come down,
but nothing can dampen
the way I feel.
The sound of our voices cheering
together
makes my spirit soar.

I float above the ground
for a brief moment,
and then my feet come back down
and touch the earth.
I am ready
to put our plan
into action.

PREPARING

The stack of firewood grows tall.
We've never had this much.
Baba arranges neat piles,
big ones at the bottom,
smaller ones above them.
And on the very top,
some still damp from yesterday's rain.

"We need extra," he says,
dusting off his hands.
"I want to be prepared in case
your auntie and the rest of the family come."

But Baba doesn't look at me
because his eyes would tell
the truth.
What if they never come?

WAITING

"I heard there was trouble today."
Khaled says as he pulls splinters
from his cricket bat after dinner.
Baba coughs on his betel treat.
"Some men stopped us on the road,"
he says when his throat clears.

Baba looks to see if Mama is listening.
"They said they need firewood as well,
they're not our trees to cut down.
And we take too many fish from the sea."

Mama has taken to trying on her nose rings
and polishing her wedding jewelry.
She puts down a small silver stud
and looks at Baba.
"Is it true, they said this?"

Baba nods. "But we have to eat,
just like them.
What can we do?"
He starts to raise his voice,

and flecks of spit land on his lips.
"There is no difference," he continues.
"We are all men with families to feed,
we are all the same in God's eyes."

Baba sighs, and in a low voice,
he mutters to himself.
All he's trying to do
is make a life for us here.
But really,
Baba is waiting to go home.
We all are.

RECORD

With a bundle of firewood
tucked under each arm,
Me, Khaled, Mama, and Baba
leave our house.
Baba says Habib,
a man who lives in the camp,
needs wood,
and we're out of rice,
so we meet by the trees outside town,
to exchange goods,
and Habib tells us stories.

Khaled brings his notebook
to record new things,
even though I told him
to leave it at home.
His pockets are small,
and it takes two hands
to carry the wood.
But Khaled balances it
on top of a pile, saying
if no one writes our stories down,

how will anyone know,
how will anyone remember?

Habib talks about
food and water given by aid agencies.
Even medical supplies.
The things we struggle for
or have no access to.

Mama looks at Baba
and makes a *tsk-tsk* sound.
Baba needed medicine
when he hurt his back.
But since we live outside the camp,
seeking a doctor's help is
next to impossible.

Khaled's fingers must ache,
he writes so fast,
barely pausing the flow of words
and sketches.
Of course he needed to bring his notebook!
But I won't admit out loud
he was right.

Habib goes back to the camp
after we wish him well,

and Baba and Khaled decide
to go to mosque,
to pray for a speedy return
to a Burma with rights for all.
"Good idea!" says Mama,
and she insists the two of us
carry the rice.

Before he sets off with Baba,
Khaled gives me his notebook and pencil
to take home.
I look for a clean, dry spot
to put them in
while I help Mama
arrange the rice bags.
A nearby tree trunk with a knothole
is the perfect place
for Khaled's treasures.

"Sticky rice tonight, Samira?"
Mama's eyes glisten.
As if she has to ask!
With two small bags each,
we go home,
bellies rumbling,
faces smiling.

MISSED OUT

A bad dream steals from my day.
Khaled has left for work.
I even missed my reading lesson,
and I'm late for the breakfast rush on the beach.
Mama hands me my bucket.

When I pass the beachside cafés,
I notice Tariq hanging on a corner,
staring at customers
who eat crispy hilsa and biryani
and sip chilled lemon sharbat.

I stand under a tree in case of rain.
Smudges of gray, at first in the distance,
grow darker and closer
until a marbled sky hangs over me.
On the water
in the distance I see Nadia
ride a waist-high wave.
Maya watches her from the lineup, too.

Out of the wave zone,
Rubi sits on her board,
like it's a rowboat.
Then she leans to one side
and falls off.
After she finds her board again,
she paddles in, and I join her on the beach.
"I have some news," she calls out,
a look of joy on her face.
"It's my Mama, she's having a baby,
and since there's prize money
for the surf contest,
I can enter!
We'll need the extra money,
Mama tells me.
And I have to learn to make baby clothes!
I can't wait to be a big sister."

Rubi runs back to the water,
making big splashes with her feet.
On her way out, she passes Nadia,
who shows her where to sit
for the smaller waves.

"Your turn, Samira," Nadia calls out.
"I left your board up there for you."

Nadia points to a yellow board
facedown in the sand
when she comes closer.
"Tariq says I should watch out for you,"
Nadia adds with a big smile on her face.
"He thinks you'll be a good surfer."
We both laugh from our hearts.

I turn to get my board.
This moment
is all I've been waiting for.
To be out here
with the girls.

But Nadia wrings her hair and says,
"I have to go now.
Mama wants me home early."
I see the sadness in her face,
and I can't hide mine either.
"Wait! You have to go now?
So soon?"

"Don't want to push my luck,"
she says.
"Besides, I feel confident leaving
Rubi and Maya with you.
And I wouldn't say that

about anyone!"
I blush at Nadia's words,
and she sees.
"I'm serious." She grins.

It feels good to be trusted,
to have friends that need me.
I've been waiting
for this moment
for a long time.

GAMES

It takes forever to get out.
The waves shift.
Here one minute,
there the next.

I paddle toward them
only to discover
I'm in the wrong spot
or I'm too late.
I wait patiently,
but soon the tide swallows up
the waves.

No lines, no swell,
nothing but an expanse of sea.
Just when I think I can do this,
the waves play games.
I expect them to be one way,
but they're not.
They change constantly,
and I can't keep up.

Khaled said sometimes
the surf is bad,
and it's not worth paddling out.
I think it's always
worth it.

LETTING GO

The hardest part of surfing
is letting go
of thinking it would be easy
of listening to voices that say I can't do it
of believing I knew my body.
I had no idea that I lean more on my left foot,
that my knees lock when I stand.

But most of all,
I have to let go
of fear
because it finds me
each time I fall.
Like a mosquito in the dark,
I slap it away,
but it hides,
comes sneaking back
when I least expect it.

Every night after practicing,
my neck and arms
scream.

"Did you hurt yourself, Samira?"

Mama watches as I rub my muscles.

"I think it's from the rice bags," I say.

Can Mama see the water on me?

Can she smell the sea salt?

Can she sense I'm changing?

ANOTHER LESSON

Khaled said it would be hard.
He warned me.
And the list of all that is against me
grows.
Surfing with driving rain in my eyes.
Cool water giving me
chills and aches.
Lightning even as
rains slow down.

Nadia says it's dangerous to surf
when there's lightning,
so we stay at home.
My brother's right,
sometimes the surf is just
bad.

WHAT IF?

"You can't give up like that!"
Aisha sounds angry,
like she's telling me off.
But she doesn't mean it.

Mama and Baba are out,
so I grab the flyer
and place it on my lap.

A rip in the roof
lets in sunlight.
Big bright letters
shine back at me.
The letters that pulled on me
when Khaled brought the flyer home.

"Whenever you talk about surfing,
your eyes sparkle, Samira."
Aisha grabs my hands and smiles.
"You're tired, that's all."

I hesitate.
Can I tell her what I'm afraid
to tell myself?
I used to share everything with Sahara,
no secrets between us.
It made us both feel good.

"I'm scared, Aisha.
Nadia is such a great surfer,
and Maya works hard at it.
She's got so much energy.
Rubi has fun every time she goes out.
If I can't surf,
if I'm not good enough,
I'm not sure what I'll do.
What if I fail? What then?"

Aisha doesn't respond.
She knows how it feels to be scared.
I think of answers
to my own questions.
But the silence continues
until it feels bigger than the questions themselves.

I put the flyer back and walk Aisha to the door.
Outside, a bank of clouds,

bruised and swollen,
comes drifting from the sea,
and silver cracks flash in the skies.
Monsoon is here.

WATER TALK

Today
an invisible bubble
sits around me,
and the outside world
is in soft focus.
Even Nadia, Maya, and Rubi
are blurry.
And it's not because of the rain.

I step on sharp coral
buried in the sand,
and a corner of my toenail
chips off.
A red line along my big toe
becomes red spots
in the sand.
I ignore the blood
that normally makes me
queasy.

I lie down on the board,
and my chin hits the rail.

Not enough wax.
I find the secret wax in my bucket.
This will help.

Back in the water,
I paddle out,
thinking how on my first day,
months ago,
I couldn't even find the sweet spot
on a surfboard.

My first wave fizzles out.
The second breaks right in front of me,
white water tossing me about.
My board takes off,
and I swim hard to catch it.
My leash was too loose.

All these mishaps,
these things going wrong
are signs of the water
talking to me.

You think you want to surf?
How badly do you want it?
How much can you take, Samira?

I climb on my board,
tighten my leash,
and paddle back out.
This is my response.

WORTH IT

When a wall of water approaches,
I swing my board around
and paddle hard
until I feel a push.
It's time to stand,
but I'm too late,
too far forward.
My hand slips,
and my cheek hits the rail.
I fall in.

The girls look over.
I'm ok.
I am surfing!

Another wave comes,
but I'm in a bad spot.
A lip of water
crashes down on my back.
My nose burns
from the sea salt,
but I've had worse.

I climb back on my board
just in time to see Nadia on a wave.
She stands tall,
her knees slightly bent,
full of grace
and ease.

That's it
that's how I need to be:
calm
centered
sure.

A small wave forms.
I know this is mine.
With my weight on the tail,
I whip the board around
and paddle hard.
Turn off the voice in my head,
tune in to the rhythm of the wave,
feel its energy.

I push up with my arms.
In one flowing movement,
I stand up.
I want to scream
for all to hear,

for all to see
that I did it,
I can do it!

My board glides through the water
feet feel planted
legs are relaxed
arms loose by my side.

All those scrapes on my knees,
all those doubts in my mind.
This moment is worth it.
Free. I am free.
I can surf.

BEFORE AND AFTER

This moment is the line
between the end of one thing
and
the beginning of another.

As I cross the line
and glance back in slow motion,
I see the joyful moments
the terrifying moments
the moments that plucked at my heart.
Each one led me
to this place
that I could never
have imagined
even
in my sweetest dream.

Before, I was Samira.
Now, I am Samira the Surfer.

A FLOW

The first break in the rainstorm
becomes an invitation
to leave the house.
Our roads are mud baths for feet.
Our hill is now a slippery slide.
It takes twice as long
to get to the beach.

Since I started learning
four months ago,
a new flow has taken shape.
A never-ending cycle
of sleep, sell, surf.
Thoughts of food, money,
our uncertain future
dissolve in the water.
Being free in the waves
is what I paddle for now.

My sisters make it possible.
Aisha, who helps me sell eggs.
Nadia, Maya, and Rubi,

who help me surf.

I thank them in small ways.

But one day,

I'd like to do something

big.

FUEL FOR SURF

A pitter patter,
turns into a heavy drumming.
For seven days,
water cascades
from creases in our roof,
like water from a spout
that Mama collects
in her silver pot.
As soon as it stops,
I tell Mama I must go sell.

An extra *plop-plop* into my pot
of boiling eggs this morning.
The girls need lunch, too!
At the beach, me and Aisha make sure
each tender, shiny oval is shell-free.
Rubi slices them open,
Nadia sprinkles spices
and passes them around.
More than just food,
eggs are fuel for surf!

The girls paddle out
and ride waves in our spot,
away from other surfers.
I stretch out on the warm sand,
relaxing and taking in the moment.

A sudden rustle in the trees
sends a chill up my spine.
I know this feeling.
Back home, soldiers spied
on our every move.

I glance at the woods
where the sound came from
and double-check the beach,
both ways.
There's no one there,
hiding, studying, judging.
Tiredness makes me see things!

Grabbing my board,
I join the girls in the lineup.
The water is where I am free.
The land is where I am watched.

LAST WAVE

Today the waves
were perfect.
We cheer and embrace
before leaving the beach.
Nadia lags behind with me,
and when the others
are far away enough,
she jerks her chin
in the direction of the trees.

"You did it, Samira.
You can surf. I'm so happy for you."
Her downturned mouth
makes me think otherwise.
"I remember the feeling
of riding across the water my first time."
She closes her eyes
as if she's recalling that moment,
and when she opens them again,
I see something:

tears.
"But today I rode my last wave."

Nadia looks into the distance
as if part of her is not here,
saying these words.
I step closer.
"Why?"

Nadia tells me the reason,
and I was hoping so much
it wouldn't be this.

"Mama knows I've been secretly surfing.
She said the beach is for selling jewelry,
nothing else."

I slowly shake my head,
and words get stuck inside of me
because we all share Nadia's fate.
The not being heard,
the not having control
over what happens,
the yearning for a different life,
we all know.

I want to tell her to not listen to her mother,

but I can't.

We are both left looking

at futures

we haven't chosen.

ONLY FOUR

It doesn't feel right.
Only me, Aisha, Rubi, and Maya
float in the lake to cool ourselves
from the summer mugginess.
"Should we still meet tomorrow?" Rubi asks.
Maya looks at me,
as if it's my decision.

I told Nadia I'd let the others know
what her mother said.
She's closer with them
and has known them longer.
Maybe it was easier to share
the bad news with me.

"Will it be like this for us all?
When it's our turn to get married,
do we just stop surfing
and doing what's important to us?"
I'm not expecting anyone
to answer my questions.

Rubi bites her lip. "I miss surfing with Nadia.
She knows which waves to avoid,
where to wait for the best ones."

Maya pouts.
"You never even paid attention
when she was trying to help you."

"I did," Rubi insists,
"But sometimes she's too serious.
Anyway, surfing isn't
a competition to me."

"Stop it!" Aisha interrupts
the back and forth between
Maya and Rubi.
"It doesn't matter now.
Don't you see that?
Nadia must be so sad at home.
Even though you don't surf now
because you can't get the surfboards,
at least you can leave the house!
Nadia can't."

Without Nadia,

there are no surfboards.

But more than that,

without her,

there is no big sister.

A DIFFERENT RAMADAN

My family is not fasting this year.
We talk about it,
go around in circles.
Baba wants to fast,
but Mama says he must eat.
Her eyes wander to his bones
that stick out.
And Baba says,
if he eats, we all eat.
So, none of us will fast.

I've never heard this talk
from my parents.
Ramadan is important to them,
to us.

Khaled picks up his sleeping mat.
He's distracted by his search
for his notebook and pencil,
which are missing.
He always keeps them
in his corner

by his cricket bat.
How unlike my brother
to lose them!

"If we don't fast," Khaled finally says,
eyebrows knitted,
"can we at least celebrate Eid?"
He looks over at Baba.

Baba tells him, "We have no money
or gifts for you and Samira.
No extra food to share with the hungry."
And no family to enjoy a delicious meal with,
I know he's thinking.

"We can still have breakfast,"
I suggest. "Just the four of us."
Baba glances at Mama, and
though no words are spoken,
they decide something as parents do
in that special way
when their eyes meet.
Mama nods, and Baba declares,
"Yes, we can."

BLENDING IN

Mama's expert hands
comb through my knots,
bunch my hair into a ponytail.
Then I know why
she makes this moment cozy.

"More are coming," she says
wrapping a rubber band around my hair.
"You mean people from home, Mama?"
I crane my neck to see her face.
"Do you think Auntie will come?"
Mama shrugs.
I know she longs
to be with her sister again.
Those dark circles around her eyes
have been there so long,
they're part of her now.

Mama says she and Auntie
were always a comfort
for each other.
When they were young,

the day came when our people
were no longer recognized
as an ethnic group in Burma.
They were both too young
to understand what it meant.
"Our people demanded citizenship,
but the government
ignored our voices," Mama says.
And growing up,
they were reminded
by their parents and grandparents
of how we were left out
as if we didn't count
as if we didn't exist.

My thoughts drift to
Khaled's notebook.
These are the stories
he's been writing
documenting
drawing.
And I feel a bigger tinge of pain
in my belly
for his lost treasure.

Maybe Auntie
will help us remember.

Maybe Auntie
will be the one retelling
our history
our story
as she combs my hair.

FAMILIAR FACES

Like a gust of wind
sweeping through the market
across the beach
into cafés,
Bengalis whisper,
"More Rohingya are here."

Hollow faces arrive
by foot
by boat.
I know their look
how it feels
what it means.
That was us.
That is us.
They walk to the refugee camp
outside of town,
where they've heard
there is shelter
water
food.

But like us,
they will be turned away and have to stay
outside the main camp.
Like us, they don't want
to be here for long.
Like us, they will return
when Burma
gives back our rights.

And how many of them
have lost their Nani and Nana?
Or Mama or Baba?
I look out for faces I might know.
Maybe Sahara is here,
wearing her blue orna.

Is that Mama?
I see her standing in the crowds,
turning this way and that.
We had the same idea.
When she spots me,
her face crumples.
I know, Mama, I wonder, too.
Are they still alive?

"All we can do is hope, Samira."
Mama kisses my cheek
and turns back to the crowds,
looking for a sign of home.

DAWN

The rip in my wall reveals
a white slither shining bright
against the blue-black sky.
The moon keeps me company
on this sleepless night.

I scrape my fingers across
my secret surf wax
and pick out the stickiness
from under my nails,
to form a tiny, tiny ball.

It softens in my warm hands.
I roll it, mold it, shape it
until a crescent moon appears.
Ramadan ends,
and a new lunar month begins,
bringing with it
hope and a fresh start.

OUR EID

Baba's milky cha drips from high.
Its sweet smell wakes me up.
Tap-tap, eggs against the rim of a bowl.
Omelet?
Slosh-slosh, water running over shrimp.
Special omelet?
These are sounds of
our first Eid in Bangladesh.

After breakfast, Baba says
we can watch the boys' game of cricket.
"I'd like to try batting!"
Does Baba know how to play?
Mama's voice is full of pride.
"He'll pick it up quickly, you'll see."
Just like my reading English.

No gifts
no silk ribbon
no oil rubbed in my hair
no fancy sequined top
no family gathering.

We've never had an Eid
like this,
and though we miss family back home,
we celebrate in a different way.
We have each other.
And I am thankful
and happy
we are together.

LOST

Khaled insists I move my sleeping mat
to see if his notebook and pencil
are there.

We only see the contest flyer
in its hiding place.
I quickly cover my secret
so Mama and Baba don't discover it.

Khaled lets out a big sigh.
With nothing to write on,
my brother has been grumpier.

"I'll check outside
where you've been teaching me
to read.
Maybe I left them there," I say.
Khaled storms off, shouting,
"The rain will have washed them away.
They'll be gone!"

I search the grass outside our house
and even go down the hill,
taking extra-long zigzags.
But I don't see them
and all I feel is Khaled's frustration
and my own.
I lost his treasures.

ABSENCE

With the rain slowing down
and the sun shining bright,
we decide to swim.
Rubi is lookout girl today.
She steps toward the open beach
and sneezes.
"We should have never let her go,"
Maya complains.
"She's noisy, and she's nowhere near
as good as Aisha."

Maya looks through the trees,
her eyes blinking rapidly,
like she's anxious.
She grabs two bunches
of hair and pulls them
in opposite directions
to tighten her high ponytail.
"Where is Aisha?
Rubi will get us all in trouble.
This was a mistake."
"It's not," I insist.

"Rubi can do it.
She just needs practice."

I never planned
on being the peacemaker,
but for weeks now,
Rubi and Maya fight.
How can things get so
out of balance when
one person leaves a group?

I hear leaves crunch
in the near distance.
"Aisha!" Maya calls out,
almost jumping with joy.
"I wish you'd come sooner."

"I overslept."
Aisha is winded.
"And I had to refill my plastic bag
with chips."
She sets her bag by a tree.
"No Rubi today?"

I point to the beach.
"She's keeping watch."
But just then, Rubi leaves her spot

and makes her way to us.

"I *think* I saw two men in uniforms,"

she announces.

"But I'm not sure."

Maya lets out a heavy sigh

and sinks to the ground.

"I knew it was a bad idea

to let you go."

Inside, I count to ten

because this silliness

is testing my patience.

ADD UP

"Look, this has to stop."
I feel three pairs of eyes
on me immediately.
"Arguing is a waste of time!
Do you know what we should do instead?
Plan to get Nadia back."

Rubi kicks a small pile of leaves.
"I agree," she says. "It's not the same
without her."

Maya's eyes fill with sadness.
"She's never coming back, you know.
I bet she's so bored at home."

"Why don't we talk to her parents?"
Aisha settles on a tree stump.
"We could try, at least."

Maya sighs.
"What should we say?
What would work?

Do you have any ideas?"
She perches on the stump next to Aisha.
"It'll be hard to change their minds.
Why would they let her
come back to the beach?"

Rubi paces back and forth,
arms folded.
"I know her mother's worried about
Nadia ruining her clothes.
How about we tell her I can fix them
if they get ripped?
She doesn't know
I've been mending them
all this time."
Then Rubi stops in her tracks.
"I can even make her something new.
My mama can show me how.
I need to practice
making clothes for the baby.
I'll tell her parents:
Nadia will have new clothes,
simple, but new!"

Aisha's eyes flash like she's had an idea.
"Yes, and Nadia's a strong swimmer.
We'll tell them she can help

if anyone gets caught in the rip current.
She's knows the conditions
better than anyone.
The contest needs her."

"That's true," Maya says,
a gentle tone in her voice.
"And we can even ask Tariq
to talk to them.
With the promise of a new job,
he might be willing to help.
If he tells them she should surf,
they might listen."

I start pacing now
because a lot of little ideas
can add up.
Nadia's parents need to know
she's valuable
she's needed
she can do more than sell jewelry.
We can't stand by
and let this happen.
It's worth trying,
for Nadia's sake
and ours.

CLICK

"But there's just one thing."
Maya's eyes wander
to me and then Aisha.
"I think only me and Rubi
should talk to her parents."

I must have given her a puzzled look.
"What I mean is. . . ," Maya searches for words.
"It's probably easier for us
when they're already angry
and on edge."

Aisha gets up from the tree stump
and clears her throat,
like she's trying to tell me something.
Then it clicks.

I remember a long time ago,
right before I met Nadia and Tariq,
I overheard some women
talking at the market.
One of them was their mother.

She has long limbs just like them,
and Tariq has the same eyes,
big and round.
She was worried about us taking
jobs and food.

I imagine her seeing
two Rohingyas on their doorstep
when they believe we're already
making their lives harder
by living in their town.
Heat rises to my cheeks,
but I quickly push it down
and say, "If it means there's a better chance
of getting Nadia back,
then we'll stay behind.
You and Rubi go
first thing tomorrow,
when they're all home."

Aisha nods.
And we all know,
we may have just avoided
a possible disaster.

With the air between us
less tense

and a plan of action

in place,

we can all get to selling our wares.

Maya asks, "Will you check for police, Aisha?"

But she's seconds late.

Aisha, plastic bag in hand,

already creeps toward the beach.

She crouches behind tall grass

like a lion hiding

from its prey.

"See, that's how you do it,"

Maya whispers to Rubi.

Rubi gives her smirk and says,

"Is this what it's like

to have a sibling?"

CLOSER

Tonight I have the jitters,
not just because of
our plan to get Nadia back.
We're calling home again,
and I can barely wait.
Mr. Ali said we could borrow his phone
since the last call was so short.

"It's fully charged!" Khaled reassures me
as he checks the screen
for the fifth time.
"Why don't you make the call, Samira?"
Baba makes the best suggestion.

Mama finishes pouring cha,
and while it cools,
we settle in.
"I'll tell you the numbers."
Khaled's hands are steady,
but mine shake.

With each number,
I get closer and closer.
With the last one in,
I clear my throat and wait.
I hear nothing but noise
like distant rain on a tin roof.
Khaled listens,
then hangs up and tries himself.
Baba takes a turn.
Maybe Mama can get through.

After several attempts,
we stop.
A chilling feeling
fills our house,
like we're untethered,
slowly drifting to a place
we don't want to visit.

"What does the scratchy noise mean?"
Since no one tells me, I have to ask.
Baba is slow to respond,
as though he's feeling for an answer.
He finally says what I want to believe.
Their phone is broken or
they've forgotten to charge it.

Mama says something
I choose to believe.
They're on their way here.

At night, Khaled
is restless,
barely sleeping.
I know he yearns
for his notebook and pencil.
How could I lose them?

I close my eyes
and pray I find them
and that Mama is right,
our family is coming.

DOWN AND UP

My eyelids are heavy,
and slowly I drift off
to the sound of waves crashing.

In my dream,
I fight against the current
to stay with the pack.
A deep ache in my neck,
tightness in my back,
my body is already tired.

An offshore breeze feathers
the tops of the breaking waves.
I see one coming, so I paddle,
but my arms are giant pitchforks,
and my board, a huge barge.

A curtain of water
doubles up
and crashes down on me.
A sharp smack to my temple,
swirling down, down I go

my nose burning,
my mouth, then stomach
filling with gritty water.

And on the beach,
a figure calls
my name,
over and over.
It looks like Baba,
but it can't be.
He never comes to the beach.
I wake up,
soaked in sweat,
a hint of my dream
on my lips.

WIN-WIN

As we approach the market,
Aisha whispers to me,
"It doesn't look good."
Rubi chews on her cheek.
A pale-faced Maya
paces back and forth.
We meet them at a T-shirt stall
and learn how our little ideas
for getting Nadia back
added up
to a whole lot of nothing.

"And Tariq didn't help," Maya tells us.
"He says Nadia has strong competition."
He can't mean me, I think.
Rubi runs her fingertips
over the sequins of a T-shirt.
"And when we left," she says,
"Nadia started folding laundry,
and I saw her shoulders shaking."
"But we can't give up," insists Aisha.
"Let's think of something else."

"Hi, Samira," comes a familiar voice
on the other side of the stall.
"I didn't see you there, Mr. Ali."
I introduce the girls and add,
"I've heard you're making food
for the surf contest."

"That's right." Mr. Ali's face beams.
"We get all our ingredients
from this market.
But today I'm doing this kind of shopping."
Mr. Ali sets down two big bags
full of T-shirts, hats, and towels.
"Which stall has the best deal for jewelry,
do you know?" he asks, wiping his brow
with a handkerchief.
"I need bracelets and necklaces."

"Our friend's an expert," says Rubi,
a glum look on her face.
"But she's at home."

"Are they gifts, Mr. Ali?" Maya asks,
her voice full of curiosity.
"Yes, they're for the goody bags.
Every competitor gets one."

Mr. Ali's words spark an idea.
In my mind, I picture the bags,
each with a T-shirt, hat, and towel.
And also, a piece of glittering jewelry
bought from Nadia.

DETAILS

But I'm not the only girl
who's on to something.
With a look of hope in her eyes,
Rubi asks Mr. Ali,
"Could our friend sell her jewelry
to the organizers?"

"As long as her parents agree.
That helps me out a lot," he replies.

We tell Mr. Ali about Nadia,
and he says he remembers the name
because her brother will help
sell food at the contest.

"Even kids who don't surf
are signing up," Mr Ali adds.
"We have fifteen so far.
I guess they heard about the goody bags."
And he laughs from deep in his belly.

Maya and Aisha exchange looks,
then whisper to each other,
as if they're adding
up the numbers.

Nadia sells her jewelry to the organizers.
Money!
She sells to the spectators on contest day.
Money!
Nadia collects the winning prize.
More money!

"Can you talk to her parents soon?"
A sweat mustache forms
on Mr. Ali's upper lip.
"I've done enough shopping today."

Rubi's face beams.
"Of course," she says.
"What a relief! It's agreed, then.
You can find me at Seaview Hotel café."
Mr. Ali lets out a big sigh
and turns to leave the market.

There's a lot of taka to make or lose.
Nadia's parents need to know this.

How can they refuse now?
They have to let her enter.

The four of us decide
Rubi and Maya will return to Nadia's,
and we'll meet in the morning to see
if the goody bag scheme
brings our big sister
back to the beach.

HOPEFUL

When I leave the woods,
something
on a tree trunk
catches my eye.

It's the contest flyer,
but unlike Khaled's,
this one is big
and has color.
Title in red,
prize money in green,
G-I-R-L-S in orange,
and is that glitter
I see?

The colors
flash like a bright flare
on a dark night.
It makes me excited
nervous
worried
all at the same time.

We need Nadia back,

we need boards,

and, most of all,

we need to ride waves.

VISION

I take long, slow steps
down our hill this morning.
It gives me time to go over
the details in my mind.
Why would our plan fail?
Why would they say no?
This might not change Nadia's fate,
but at least she could surf
for a little while longer.

I rub my eyes with my knuckles,
because I must be seeing things.
Past the fishermen
who throw their nets out to sea
are three girls.
Rubi and Maya stand on the beach
with Nadia!
They have surf boards with them!

Aisha sits in the shade
arranging their wares,

and when she spots me,
she waves, and together
we run to the others.
The five of us hold hands
and spin in circles
until we sink into the sand,
breathless and dizzy.

Nadia tells us
how Mr. Ali bought jewelry,
lots of it.
And when he saw her brother,
they shook hands in agreement
to seeing Tariq on contest day
to helping prepare food
to trying him out
for a possible job
if they're a suitable match.

"And you should have seen Baba," Nadia tells us.
"His chest puffed out.
And Mama, grinning all morning.
As soon as Mr. Ali left,
she counted the money
three times
and closed her eyes to thank God!"

Rubi makes a trunk with her arm
and trumpets like an elephant.
Aisha twirls
while Maya claps her hands
and skips along the beach
with Nadia.
I sit on the sand,
watching the girls
celebrate.
Right now,
it feels like we're invincible,
like our bond is even stronger,
like nothing in this world
can ever tear us apart.

COMMIT!

In these past six months,
I've learned many lessons.
Go while it's good.
Knee-high, glassy waves
break in sets of four.
"See that tree on the beach?"
Nadia points to the tallest tamarisk.
"It lines up with the waves today.
That's how you know where
to paddle back out to."

Maya shows me how to be
quick to stand.
Push up, knees bent, legs strong.
Training your arms and legs does help,
I see that now.
"Most of all, commit," she says.
I repeat it as I try.
Commit!
"Look where you're going!
Not at your feet!"
These tips stick with me,

in my bones,
my muscles.

When I'm on a wave,
time slows down.
There is no thinking.
There is only being.

Me
my board
and the water
meet in a playful dance.

I lean on the rail,
and the board turns.
My weight comes back to center,
and the board straightens.

Wind rushes past me
as the sun beats down.
I am in the moment.
This moment, right now.
All of me is here.
Nothing matters.
Not one single thing.

FOUND

Khaled holds the tarp
on our front door.
Its edges are ragged and worn
from wind and rain.
Rubi sews flecks of black stitches
making a bulky hem.
"That should stop it from ripping."
She admires her repair.
"At least until next monsoon season."

While we work outside,
Aisha comes running up the hill.
"Guess what I found," she says,
with her hands behind her back.

It must be important,
whatever it is.
Aisha is out of breath.

"Surf wax?" Khaled guesses.
Rubi taps her chin.
"A bird?"

Aisha shakes her head,
making her ponytail sway.
"I have no idea," I say. "Just tell us!"

Aisha brings her hands forward
to reveal
Khaled's notebook and pencil.

"You found them.
I can't believe it!"
Khaled's eyes go wide in disbelief
as he reaches out for his treasures.
I jump up and down with joy,
my heart pounding.

Faded and swollen
from moisture in one corner,
the cover still has his name
written in big letters on the front.

Khaled presses them to his chest
and gives thanks to God
for answering his prayers.
I silently thank him
for answering mine as well.

Rubi looks confused,
but she'll have to wait
for an explanation.
I'm too giddy
to tell her why writing
is so important to my brother.

"Where did you find them?"
Khaled flips through the notebook,
making sure the words and pictures
are intact.

"I was out collecting bamboo
to put on our roof,
and I saw them tucked
in the knothole of a tree."

Then I remember I left them there,
in a dry, safe place
when Khaled and Baba
went to mosque
and me and Mama
took rice home.
It *was* me who lost them.

I give Aisha a tight squeeze.
She saved me and my brother!
I'll sleep well tonight
and so will Khaled,
because his notebook and pencil are back,
because his time with Nana is back
even if it's just a dream.

MY TURN

I watch the water for a moment,
decide where to paddle out.
The waves are shifting today,
breaking in one spot
and then another.
But they're smaller,
and that's better for me.
Wait a little, I tell myself.
Save my energy,
for when I need it most.

I'm covered in bruises and scrapes,
filled with tips and experience.
The things I have learned
have shaped me into a surfer.

When I see it's good,
I paddle out,
taking my time getting to the lineup.
Slow and steady, I tell myself.

Find a point of reference on the beach,
face the horizon,
read the energy of the swell.

Dark lines form in the water.
Waves are coming.
Go for this one or wait?
I let it pass.
The wave builds, then dumps
in one crash of white water
where it's shallow.
Another goes by.
The waves arrive in threes,
the next one is the last in this set.

Water begins to rise in a long wall.
It stands tall, in one mass,
thick and wide.
This is the one.
I paddle, keeping an eye over my shoulder
in case the wall shifts.
It comes closer, my strokes deepen,
in one propelling motion,
pushing down,
pulling back.
In an instant,
I am up

and riding.

When I come in,

I see a figure walk off.

The long legs and arms

give him away.

Tariq.

THANK YOU

"Let's go, Samira,
we're running late," Khaled calls out.
Baba stands by the door,
adjusting his clean cap.
Mama puts on Nani's nose ring.

We are going to the café
to thank Mr. Ali
for the use of his phone.
It was Baba's idea,
and Mama agreed immediately.

Baba shakes Mr. Ali's hand
to thank him
to accept his help
to welcome friendship.
Mr. Ali wipes a table
and motions for us to sit.
We take our seats as he pours
cha into five tall glasses.

I sip and glance
at the flower stand
across the street
and spot Tariq
quietly watching us.
As Mr. Ali spoons
rasgulla into bowls,
Tariq's face turns gloomy,
and his cheeks flush bright red.
I know he wants
what we're about to enjoy:
his most favorite dessert.

ANSWERS

Overnight, the beach has become
a small village of white tarps
stretching over frames,
tables and beach chairs arranged in a line.

A banner gives the village a name.
"Cox's Bazar Surf Contest."
This new buzz, easy to catch,
sends sparks through my body.

One of the organizers calls me over.
She puts down her cardboard box
full of jerseys and flyers.
"Are you one of the girls who surfs?"
the lady asks.
My smile responds for me.
"You'll need this!" she says,
thrusting a paper and pencil in my hand.
"It's an entry form."

I instinctively take it,
because this is what I want, right?

It's what I've been working toward, right?
I'm ready to compete, right?
With each rising question,
the answer appears,
and it's the same one every time.
Yes, yes, yes!

Thanks to Khaled, I can read
most of the words,
enough to know how to fill it out.
As I write, an idea comes to me.
I ask the lady for three more forms,
then head home,
humming along the way.

GOLD

In my hands,
three contest entry forms.
In Aisha's hands,
one small yellow pencil.
Today, we don't need buckets
or surfboards.
"What's this meeting about, Samira?
What couldn't wait?"
Nadia squats across from me.
Rubi and Maya sit beside her,
curiosity on their faces.

I hand them the papers.
"I thought I could help you
fill in the contest forms."
Each girl stares at the sheets
like they're gold.
"This is so exciting!"
Maya's nose wrinkles.
"How do you fill it out?
What does this say?

Wait, let me guess.
Does it say *name*?"

Rubi drops her paper,
and we all watch
as a gust of wind
takes it straight into
a muddy puddle
by a coconut palm.
Rubi rushes over.
"Oh no," she cries, brushing mud
from the writing.
Then she giggles,
"Never mind, I can't read it anyway."
Rubi's jokes always help
turn a bad thing into a good thing.

As we fill out the forms,
Aisha feeds us.
She passes around chips,
handfuls to me, Nadia, and Rubi,
and a stack of three to Maya,
who smiles in return.
Even though Aisha's not competing,
we're a group.
We do things together.

I read out each line.

Nadia lets Rubi and Maya go first.

They share the pencil.

And soon,

with letters that slant

this way and that,

three forms are filled out.

We are one step closer

to competing

in the surf contest.

ANOTHER PLACE

Wrapped in Nani's blanket,
I flick through Khaled's magazine
until I find a surfer girl
and imagine that she's me.
Then I close my eyes,
and pushed by each gentle wave,
I drift off to another place.

LAST PERSON

I sweep the floor,
thinking about what I'd buy
with the prize money.
More food, new clothes,
a cell phone.
A notebook for Khaled.
A new comb for Mama,
and even a fancy hijab.
She's given some of hers to the women
who left theirs behind in Burma.
And for Baba?
A new cap and spit bowl.

My imaginary gift-giving stops
when Khaled puts his notebook aside
and opens the front door.
He invites in the last person
I expect to see and says,
"I'll see you tomorrow, right?"
Tariq doesn't answer.
His eyes search for what—who—he has come for.

"You can't do it!"
He yells, pointing at me.
"What's this all about?"
Khaled cuts him off.
Mama grabs her hijab
and covers her head.
Baba is up on his feet in a flash.
"What are you accusing Samira of?"
His voice a siren so loud,
I'm sure the neighbors can hear it.

Tariq doesn't answer.
Instead, he continues shouting.
"I'll tell the authorities.
I'll tell everyone.
And you Rohingyas will be sent back."
Disbelief flashes across Khaled's face.
"You'd turn us in? Tariq, I trusted you."

Baba steps forward.
"Wait, sit down," he says, calmer now.
"Let's talk."
But Tariq ignores the invitation.
"You people are taking everything from us,
our jobs, our firewood.
Even the food in our cafés."

My mind flashes to yesterday
when Tariq watched us eat and drink
with Mr. Ali.

"Now surfing," Tariq continues.
"I've watched you competing with Nadia
for waves and now
for the prize money."

Me? Serious competition
for Nadia?
I am nowhere near
as good a surfer as she is.
And just as I think things
can't get any worse,
Tariq says,
"Pull out of the surf contest
or I'll talk.
Your choice, Samira!"

Mama lets out a cry.
My secret
is no longer mine.

WEB

My blood boils,
and my hands form fists,
ready to pound on his chest.
"We all know Nadia's going to win, Tariq,
Not me!
I just like being out there.
You can't take that away!"

This outburst will ruin my family.
Leave Bangladesh and return to Burma?
Fear for our lives all over again?
Tariq points his finger at me
like it's a dagger.
"You have tonight to think about it,
then you'll see what's coming to you."

I'm left speechless
as seconds pass.
Tariq's been watching me.
The phantom at the beach was real.
It was Tariq,
hiding in the trees,

spying on me
when I was learning to surf.

"You have until the morning."
Tariq spits out words,
then leaves,
his threat fouling the air.
And I am left trapped
in a web
of tightly woven lies.

His.
And mine.

INSIDE OUT

Mama's crying sends me folding
into my own heap of despair.
"Why, why?" She sobs.
"Why did you do this?"
Baba's hug doesn't calm her.
Instead, her wails get louder.

It feels like my bare hands
are holding up the banks
of a flooding river.
I turn to use my back,
my whole body, to stop the collapse,
but the banks crumble
and go with the current.
There's nothing I can do but
surrender, give up,
let go of it all.

I sit down on the mat
and tell Mama and Baba
everything.

My secrets flip inside out.
All that I have been hiding,
guarding close to me
is open for them to see.

GONE

I go behind my parents' backs
not to disobey.
It's to make something for us,
to help us,
to give us a new beginning.

I tread water in what has become
a flooded river
and look around for debris,
a branch,
anything to hold.

"Mama, the prize money is Tk.10,000.
It could change our lives."
For a second, I think she hears me,
understands my actions.
I grip on to hope like it's a branch
that will save me.
But Mama says, "Khaled could win.
You don't have to do the contest."

But I'm better than Khaled!
Baba's voice rattles in my mind,
Only a boy can change a family's fate.

"That's why you practice every day?"
Baba tips his head to one side,
like he just worked something out.
How does he know?
Mama's eyes grow big.
"You knew about this?"
"I was curious," Baba admits.
"Samira spends more time at the beach
than it takes to sell eggs.
I followed her and saw her surfing."

The phantom, it wasn't Tariq,
it was Baba!
He's been watching me
all this time!

Mama's jaw goes slack,
and blood drains from her face.
She gives Baba an icy look.
"You didn't tell me."

Baba hesitates, then explains.
"I thought it would be too hard for her.

That she wouldn't stick with it."
He pauses, then a bright glimmer
crosses his face.
"But she got better.
And to see my Samira smile like that again."
Head in hands, Baba joins Mama on the floor.
"I didn't know she'd entered the contest.
That brings too much risk."

Eyes red and puffy, Mama faces me.
"The water . . . it took your Nani and Nana."
I look down at my feet.
The branch I cling to
rips away, inch by inch,
from the collapsing bank.

Khaled puts his arm around Mama.
"Samira can surf well.
She has a good chance."
But he is met with a scowl.
"And you are also to blame.
You helped your sister do this.
We trusted you to take care of her."

I look at Mama, and I'm sure I see
a new line on her brow.
And it's my fault.

"Samira, it is not even a question.
Tariq will report us.
Our lives will be thrown into turmoil
again."

Baba adds,
"You will not surf, and you will not compete.
It's safer for you and us if you don't."
His words snap the branch
I cling to.
They are
my end.

DIVIDED

Minutes pass or maybe hours,
I don't know which.
Our house is divided.
Our lives turned upside down.
One minute, fear suffocates me.
What was I thinking, risking everything?
Just because the water calls me,
tempts me to dare to live a different life.
The next minute, the wave breaks, and courage springs up,
making me feel brave.
I can put it all back together again.
If only given a chance.

ADRIFT

Khaled and Baba serve dahl at dinnertime,
Me and Mama stare at our plates.
Like rafts cut adrift,
each of us alone, helpless.
And it is all my doing.

Not surfing in the contest,
giving up what I love,
what I believe can help our family,
this is not what I wanted.

Khaled kneels by Mama
and holds her hands in his.
"You should see Samira riding waves, Mama.
Her arms know how to paddle, when to push up."
Khaled's face brightens.
"She's a natural."
He looks at Mama and Baba and waits.
His efforts are wasted.

My ears are ringing,
my bones aching.
I am exhausted,
we all are.

CHANGE

The music of our mornings
is replaced by a somberness.
All of me is weary
and numb.
I go to Mama and Baba
and say what I must.
They are right.
I can't surf in the contest today.
It risks too much.
I'm sorry.

Back in my corner,
I wrap my orna extra tight around my head,
tucking in loose strands.
Khaled packs wax for the contest.
That
hurts.
He's allowed to surf,
Mama and Baba say,
because people
accept boys surfing.

"I tried, Samira. I really did.
I'm sorry. I just . . ."
Khaled understands
what I'm going through.

Untruths slip out of my mouth.
"It's ok.
It's for the best."
I try to force a smile, but it won't come.
"Promise me one thing," I add.
"That you'll fill the pages in your notebook
with what it's like to surf.
Write about it, draw pictures
so I'll never forget how it feels."

A quick nod from Khaled
confirms that was already his plan,
as though he needs to get it down on paper,
for both of us.

He turns to leave, and
only then do I hear something.
It takes me a few seconds
to recognize the voice.
Aisha is outside, calling me,

her voice close to cracking.

Me, Khaled, Mama, and Baba rush to the door.

"Come to the beach, quick!

There's trouble at the contest."

ALL OR NONE

The girls stand huddled together,
their orange contest jerseys
lit like torches in the early morning.
But their mood is dark.
Maya and Rubi stand with their arms crossed,
Nadia, hands on her hips, talks with them.

Contest organizers on their cell phones
walk this way and that,
scratching their heads.
The boys sit under the tarps.
Some wax their boards
some stretch
some watch the surf.

There are no smiles or jokes.
The air is not buzzing
with anticipation.
This is not how I imagined
a surf contest would be.

We come closer and hear Nadia.
"We won't take part in this contest."
That can't be right!
"Not one of us." Rubi's voice is stern.
"It's all the girls or none."
Maya agrees with her.
"It's not fair if Samira doesn't surf.
There's no other way.
We'll only surf if she does."

All of this because of me?

Nadia's mother sits in the shade

next to a woman with
a baby bump.
She must be Rubi's mother.
And Maya, I wonder how she feels.
Only her parents
are not here.

The spectators, restless,
chatter amongst themselves.
A few gather their towels and bags
and start to leave.
Khaled walks over to the boys,
and they whisper.

"That includes the boys!"
he calls out.
"Now they're saying
they won't surf if the girls don't."

MY WELL

I need some air—
this crowd is stifling.
Mama and Baba follow me.
A safe distance away,
I look straight into their eyes,
let them both see the depth of my well.

"Baba, you once told me to keep my eyes ahead.
That's what I'm doing.
Mama, you say Khaled is our only chance,
but he's not.
I am, too.
Let me show you."

I sink into the sand,
let the grains cake my hands
and legs.
I am a few feet away from the water,
and all I want is to be
in it.

RELEASE

Mama bends down,
reaching for my hand.
She pulls gently, encouraging me
to stand up.
A calm fills her,
softening her brow,
relaxing her mouth.
"If your Nani and Nana were here,"
she says, "they'd want to see you surf."
And now her eyes grow glassy.
"And we do as well.
We want to see our brave Samira surf."
Mama kisses my cheek.
In her touch,
I feel Nani's blanket
and hear Nana's voice.

"You've worked hard, Samira,"
Baba smiles, showing me his
red teeth.
"You deserve this."

A giant boulder rolls off my chest,
and suddenly I can breathe again.
Did I hear right?
They're letting me surf?
I throw my arms around Mama,
hugging her extra long.
I know how hard this is for her,
how fear brushes up against her each day,
how she is letting go of a little part of me.
When I release Mama,
she leans on Baba.
"Be safe, Samira," she says.

Khaled must have seen us,
because he walks over.
"Take mine," he offers,
handing me his board.

"But you need the wax," Baba says.
"The one in your bucket."
How did Baba find out?
"I know it helps you stay on the board.
Did I get you the right one?"
Baba laughs when he sees me
slowly realizing the truth.

I hug my full-of-surprises Baba
who is good at keeping secrets,
like me.
And he reassures me,
"As soon as this contest ends,
I will speak with Tariq.
If his parents knew how Khaled
has been a good friend
and how you've helped
Nadia with jewelry sales,
they might think differently."

He found out about the goody bags?
What does Baba not know?

Khaled gives me his wax
and wishes me luck
as the contest organizer calls out,
"It's on!"

The crowd cheers,
and surfers clap their hands
on their boards.
Cox's Bazar Surf Contest
is about to begin.

CONTEST RULES

1. The horn blows once, and a green flag means go.
2. Surf for fifteen minutes.
3. The horn blows twice, and a red flag means end of heat.

The combined points from your best two waves make up your final score.

SHARE

I duck under the water
and forget my worries.
The sea is my teacher,
and today it is my friend,
my joy.

I head to the lineup with the girls
as the world around me
slows
down.

A big, deep breath,
a scan of the water.
Swell is coming,
I feel it.

I focus on a bumpy line on the horizon.
Soon, a rippled wall rises,
and I paddle as hard as I can.

My board thrusts forward,
and I take off
in one fluid motion,
gliding up and down the open face.
I am in heaven,
where there is no separation
between the wave
my surfboard
and me.

The heat has plenty of rides
for each of us.
We girls share something else now:
our very first surf contest.
The best wave,
Nadia takes it.
She zips across the face
as spectators cheer.

After the horn sounds twice
and the red flag is raised,
we paddle in.

My whole body tingles from
dreaming to surf
the learning I've done
the knocks I've taken
the joy I feel
riding waves
in Cox's Bazar Surf Contest.

ANNOUNCEMENT

On the beach, I am still flying.
"Well done! We're so proud of you,"
Mama and Baba call out,
their faces radiant.
Rubi and Nadia's mothers clap.
Aisha hugs me extra tight.

As the boys' heat begins,
we settle in to watch
and support.
Chatter ripples through the crowd.
Competitors dance to music,
singing and laughing.
Some snack on mangoes
or even drink sodas,
celebrating this special day.
This is what I thought
a surf contest would look like.

When lunchtime arrives,
Mr. Ali hands out small boxes of
steamed rice and vegetable curry to surfers.

Tariq sells the extras to spectators.
He's so busy, our eyes never meet.
Or maybe he's avoiding me.
Baba says we'll talk to him later,
and my heart pounds at the thought.

Then, over the loudspeaker:
"And the winner of the girls' division . . ."
I weave in and out of the crowd,
looking for Nadia.
As her name is called out,
some surfers,
upset with the results,
cry and storm off.
I might have, too,
if I didn't know Nadia.

I finally see Aisha, Rubi, and Maya,
hands in the air,
jumping,
and Nadia cheering in the middle.

She is handed a giant poster board,
on it a check for Tk.10,000
and a golden statue
of a surfer on a wave.

Her mama and baba

blush as they watch her

become the center of attention.

Click, click, click,

a photographer takes photos of Nadia.

And one of all of us,

arms linked.

We'll never forget this day.

FAMILY TIME

To be here with Mama and Baba is
my victory,
my trophy.
My mama's face is bright and happy,
like it used to be.
"Nani and Nana are saying,
Of course Samira surfs.
She is brave and strong."

Baba boasts to a spectator,
"My daughter learns quickly.
She just started surfing,
but she's a natural."

Khaled takes third place
in the boys' division.
He congratulates me on competing
and not getting hurt,
then pokes me in the rib.
Always teasing!

I could never have done it
without him.
He helped me
took risks for me
believed in me.
He showed me that
taking care of myself,
however that looks,
is important.

And now I know,
to help my family,
I can sell eggs.
And to feel alive and happy,
deep down inside,
I can take to the water and surf.

ENCIRCLE

Contest organizers slowly fold banners
and roll up tarps
as the crowds break apart.
Mr. Ali invites everyone back
for the next contest.
"Don't forget to invite your friends," he says,
handing out goody bags.

Rubi opens hers and pulls out a T-shirt.
She runs her fingers over the stitching
and smiles.
I wonder if a new sewing project
is brewing in her mind.

"Who knows, if I practice hard,
maybe I'll win a surf contest
one day," Maya says,
taking a shell necklace
from her goody bag.
It's one that Nadia
sold to Mr. Ali.

Maya unlocks its silver clasp
and wraps the necklace around
the bun she has scooped her hair into.
I tell her how pretty it looks,
and she smiles and adds,
"And you never know,
my parents might watch me."
Although Maya jokes,
I hear a hint of sadness
in her voice.

It's not hard to imagine her
waving a gold trophy in the air.
She's determined
and works hard.
Though I don't see her parents
in this picture,
for Maya's sake,
I want to believe
anything is possible.

Nadia leaves the contest
floating on a cloud,
flanked by her mama
on one side,
clutching her prize tight,

and her baba
on the other side,
carrying her surfboard.

"Choose something
for yourself," I tell Aisha
when she peeks into my bag.
Aisha flips through a magazine
and stops on a page with a map,
surf spots marked with pins.
"I'd like this," she says.
"And Dada would, too."
She folds the corner of the page,
and I know she's already dreaming
of faraway places.
Then Aisha whispers a thank-you
in my ear.

FEAR

Under the coconut trees,
Khaled and Tariq make peace.
Khaled assured Baba
it would be best this way.

Tariq's face was pale,
Khaled tells us later.
His eyes, rimmed with dark circles.
He'd had a long day
preparing food for the contest
from the early hours of the morning,
then selling on the beach.

He apologized
for being a fool
for being mean spirited
for taking his frustrations out on me.

He thought I was making his life
more difficult.
That I'd win the contest.
And when he saw us

enjoying a drink and dessert
at Mr. Ali's café,
his anger spilled over.

He told Khaled he'd drop this threat
against us.
"See?" Khaled tells me.
"Of course," I reply.
"His sister won the contest."
While my brother may be willing to forget,
I accept the apology
and still feel angry
all at once.

I push Tariq and the hurt
out of my mind.
Instead, I think about my day.
Remembering each moment
brings me peace,
and inch by inch,
my tired limbs
melt under my blanket
as I slowly fall asleep.

STARS

Me and Aisha kneel next to her dada.
His finger hovers over the map
in the surf magazine.
And in his gravel voice,
he shares stories of these towns,
bringing each one alive.

Mama listens in, smiling
as she pours cha into six cups.
Baba rinses shrimp,
and Khaled taps eggs against a bowl.
We'll share a delicious omelet
as one big family.

"Will you teach me?" Aisha asks.
"To surf, I mean."
Our eyes meet.
Her question takes me by surprise.
"I decided I can be brave," she explains.
"Just like you."

After breakfast, I get my things ready.
Eggs and wax.
There's a small swell this afternoon.
Ideal for learning.
I tie my blue orna on my bucket,
maybe Sahara
and Auntie
and the rest of my family will come,
if not today,
then maybe tomorrow or the next day.

Nadia, Maya, and Rubi watch the waves.
Four freshly waxed surfboards
sit by them on the sand.

Behind me, there's a chatter
of excited voices,
and when I turn around,
Aisha steps out from the woods.
She's not alone.
A group of girls joins her,
some younger, some older,
mostly Bengali,
but a few Rohingya, too.
They all want to surf, they say.
Can I teach them?

Answers can be like stars.
Sometimes they're bright and clear,
sometimes they're hidden or faint.
I still have lots of questions,
many of them unanswered.
But this answer is the brightest star of all.
I step in the water,
and the lesson begins.

AUTHOR'S NOTE

While *Samira Surfs* is fictional, the journey Samira and her family undertake, from devastating loss to rebuilding life in another country, is an everyday reality for refugees.

The history of Myanmar (formerly known as Burma) is both complex and turbulent, including its time under British rule from 1824 to 1948. When the British reign came to an end, Rohingya, mostly Muslims, believed they would be granted the right to self-government. They had sided with the British during World War II, unlike the Buddhists, who were loyal to the Japanese. But Rohingya were misled by the British and were left vulnerable, powerless, and without autonomy.

This precarious situation further deepened the divisions between the country's majority Buddhist and minority Muslim population.

Although Myanmar has been home to Rohingya for many generations, they are no longer recognized as one of the official 135 ethnic groups that make up the country. This announcement, made by the government in 1982, left them without a state, citizenship, and human rights.

To this day, Myanmar regards the Rohingya as illegal

immigrants from Bangladesh, while Rohingya have reported persecution by the Myanmar military, police, and even once-friendly neighbors. In Rakhine State in northern Myanmar, where most Rohingya live, villages were set on fire, women were assaulted, and many people were brutally killed. With no sign of an end to these atrocities, many set off on perilous journeys by foot and boat to countries like Malaysia, Indonesia, Thailand, and Bangladesh. As of publication, around 860,000 refugees have made it to Bangladesh, where they settled in the Kutupalong refugee camp.

International aid agencies responded to this humanitarian crisis by offering water, food, shelter, and providing medical care for those in need. Apart from malnutrition and disease, refugees endure flooding and mudslides during monsoon season. This only further complicates and threatens their lives in the camp. The influx has also caused friction in host communities where Bangladeshi already live in impoverished conditions and struggle for basic needs.

Kutupalong camp was unofficially started around 1991. Rohingya arriving after 1992 were not allowed to register as refugees because the camp was already full. However, many set up their own shelter in makeshift camps, just like Samira's family. In 2019, the Bangladeshi government ordered the construction of barbed-wire fences, watch towers, and the installation of CCTV cameras to increase security. This move is seen by Rohingya as further mistreatment of their people. The reason I chose to set this novel in 2012 is precisely because a story like this would be nearly impossible under the most recent restrictions.

To this day, Rohingya in Cox's Bazar still dream of returning to a Myanmar that recognizes them as citizens and protects them as a people. In the meantime, they strive to educate their children, maintain their identity as an ethnic group and as individuals, and make their voices heard. Those voices come in many forms, whether it's calling for human rights, writing about their experiences, or forming support groups for the community. Perhaps it was a desire to have freedom of self-expression that inspired Nasima Akter to surf. Nasima is believed to be the first Rohingya female to brave the waves in Cox's Bazar.

A surfer myself (still learning after many years), I know the lessons the waves have taught Samira, the fears she has overcome, and the courage she has summoned to climb back on her board after each wipeout. Growing up with Muslim family on my father's side, I am aware of the barriers she has broken down by daring to surf as a girl, even though I have not experienced those barriers myself.

It is my hope that families like Samira's can find peace and empowerment. *Samira Surfs* was written to honor them and their journey home, wherever that may be.

FURTHER READING

ROHINGYA MEDIA

The online newspaper, Rohingya Post, was started in 2012 and features news sourced by Rohingya citizen journalists about the persecution of Rohingya by the Myanmar government. The website also includes information about Rohingya culture, food, music, and sport.
https://www.rohingyapost.com/category/refugee-news/

INTERNATIONAL REPORTS

https://www.aljazeera.com/news/2017/10/28/rohingya-crisis-explained-in-maps/
https://newsforkids.net/articles/2019/04/08/rohingya-refugees-people-without-a-home/

SURF CLUB

Cox's Bazar is home to a group of energetic surfers who make up Bangladesh Surf Girls and Boys Club. The club was started by the husband and wife team Rashed Alam and Venessa Rude Alam. To find out more about what they do and how you can support their efforts, please check out www.bangladeshsurfing.com.

PHOTOGRAPHY

Photojournalist Allison Joyce has captured the lives of Rohingya and Bangladeshi communities through her work, which can be viewed at http://allisonjoyce.com.

HOW TO GET INVOLVED

Humanitarian and non-governmental agencies work within refugee communities to distribute food and water, provide free legal services, and promote understanding and appreciation between cultural groups. You can read about the work these organizations do and how to get involved below.

https://www.unicef.org/emergencies/rohingya-crisis

https://www.zakat.org/our-work/where-we-work/bangladesh

ACKNOWLEDGMENTS

I wrote *Samira Surfs* with a team of brilliant people by my side. My literary agent, Wendi Gu, is nothing short of amazing. Thank you for believing in me, Wendi. I feel seen and heard by you, and that gives me the courage to write stories that live in my dreams.

My heartfelt appreciation goes to Namrata Tripathi, Zareen Jaffery, Jasmin Rubero, Sydnee Monday, and everyone at Kokila and Penguin Young Readers. I can't thank you enough for the energy and dedication you've brought to this project. From the very beginning, I knew I was in good hands.

Joanna Cárdenas, editor extraordinaire at Kokila, deserves all my gratitude. Your attention to detail, unwavering support, and gentle nudges have taught me so much on this journey. You took a chance on me, and I am forever in your debt.

Fahmida Azim, your gorgeous cover and interior illustrations make this book a visual treat. Each scene filled with your creative vision invites the reader into an intimate world and enhances their experience as the story unfolds. I applaud you for your lovely artwork.

My cousin Nadia Zaidi, you were gracious enough to answer questions late at night, taking the time to help me figure things out. We are oceans apart, but I am lucky to call you family.

I am grateful for my childhood friend Asha Khanom. Knowing I could reach out to you to triple-check a fact was not only a tremendous help, it was also an immense comfort.

While writing this book, I consulted with experts whose insights and stories were enriching to me personally and invaluable for my research. I am deeply honored that you shared your experiences and placed your trust in me. Thank you for helping me shape this book.

~ Jasmin Akhter, award-winning cricketer, voted one of BBC's 100 most inspiring and influential women of 2019, Street Child United Young Leader

~ Rashed Alam and Venessa Rude Alam, co-founders and co-directors of Bangladesh Surf Girls and Boys Club

~ Gretchen Emick, MSW

~ Haikal Mansor, co-founder of Rohingya Action Ireland and general secretary of the European Rohingya Council

~ Samira Siddique, doctoral researcher in the Energy and Resources Group, UC Berkeley

~ Raees Tin Maung, founder and board chair, Rohingya Human Rights Network, Rohingya Children's Projects

~ Nasir Zakaria, executive director of the Rohingya Culture Center of Chicago

A special thank-you must go to the three beautiful men

in my life: my husband, Leonard, and my sons, Luc and Taj. You patiently listened when I read lines out loud to see if they made sense. You politely steered me back to my computer and insisted on cooking dinner so I could continue writing. I also appreciate you not running me over in the surf or dropping in on the small waves I ride. But, most of all, I see that you genuinely understand how writing is important to me, how it sustains me. I feel your love and support every single day.